GUAPA

A play

By

Caridad Svich

Santa Catalina Editions

An imprint of NoPassport Press

GUAPA

2012, revised 2013 by Caridad Svich

Cover design: Sam Trevino. www.samdidit.com

Santa Catalina Editions
An imprint of NoPassport Press
NoPassportPress@aol.com
www.nopassport.org

ISBN: 978-1-304-67306-0

Script History:

This play was developed at and with the The Lark
Play Development Center, NoPassport theatre
alliance, Repertorio Espanol, ScriptWorks and the
2012 Teatro Vivo Latino New Play Festival. Special
thanks to José Zayas, Audrey Esparza, Maggie Bofill,
Zuri Eshun, Anne Garcia-Romero, Jorge Huerta, Alex
Koch, Flor De Liz Perez, Rey Lucas, Bernardo Cubria,
Dalia Davi, Annie Henk, Heather Helinsky, Bobby
Moreno, Martha Wade Steketee. The play was a
finalist for the 2012 Eugene O'Neill Playwrights
Center Theatre Conference.

This play received a rolling world premiere courtesy
of the National New Play Network in the 2012-2013
season at Borderlands Theatre in Arizona, Phoenix
Theatre in Indiana, and Miracle Theatre Group in
Oregon, with support, in part, from an NNPN
Collaboration Grant, and the NNPN Continued Life
Fund.

The play received a 2012 Edgerton Foundation New
Play Award.

For the Borderlands Theater, Tucson, Arizona premiere October 4-21, 2012:

Director: Barclay Goldsmith
Assistant Director: Eva Tessler
Scenic Design: Andres Volovsek
Sound Design: Jim Klingenfus
Lighting Design: Clint Bryson
Costume Design: Kathy Hurst
Technical Director: Frank Calsbeek
Video Design: Brenda Limon
Production Manager: Elizabeth Blair

Cast:

GUAPA: Gabriela Urias

ROLY: Annabelle Nuñez

PEPI: Marisa Acosta

LEBON: Mario Tineo

HAKIM: Adrian Gomez

For the Phoenix Theatre, Indianapolis, Indiana premiere January 3-20, 2013:

Director: Bryan Fonseca
Assistant Director: David Graham
Scenic Design: James Gross
Sound Design: Tim Brickley
Lighting Design: Laura Glover
Costume & Prop Design: Ashley Kiefer
Technical Director: Nolan Brokamp
Video Design: Brenda Limon
Choreographer: Mariel Greenlee
Stage Manager: Chelsey Wood

Cast:

GUAPA: Phebe Taylor

ROLY: Patricia Castañeda

PEPI: Magdalena Ramos

LEBON: Güero Loco

HAKIM: Adrian Gomez

For the Miracle Theatre Group, Portland, Oregon premiere March 21-April 13, 2013:

Director: Olga Sanchez
Scenic Design: José Gonzalez
Lighting Design: Kristeen Crosser
Sound Design: Rory Stitt
Props: Kenichi Hillis
Costume Design: Emily Powell Wright
Fight Choreographer: Kristen Mun
Master Carpenter: Collin Lawson
Scenic Painter: Mark Loring
Stage Manager: Alyssa Essman
Production Manager: Estela Robinson
Production Technician: Julie Rosequist
Graffiti Art Consultant: Chazaq Pinto
Video Design: Brenda Limon
Video Design & Production: Lucas Welsh

Cast:

GUAPA: Michelle Escobar
ROLY: Sofia May-Cuxim
PEPI: Crystal Ann Muñoz
LEBON: Pablo Saldana
HAKIM: Tristan Nieto

On GUAPA

The landscape of Caridad Svich's new play is hostile;
both literally and metaphorically. The water is toxic.
The town is isolated and dusty. Iconic symbols of the
American dream---the endless open road and railroad
tracks---are now in process of decay and threatened
by offstage violence from the border. When the
circumstances of the immediate Present provide no
hope, human nature tends to either dream of a Future
ideal society, or nostalgically look back to the Past as
a former utopia.

Svich first brings us to the familiar family
dinner table where this tension between past, present,
and future simmers and boils. Oldest son Lebón
wants to reclaim the past through his self-taught
online study of Quechua. His half-sister Pepi
nostalgically remembers the traditions of their Abuela
in Mexico. Their cousin Hakim, on the other hand,
has been left out of the American dream, accepts his
lot, remaining intensely private and complacent
within the present system of community college and
work. Matriarch Roly, who has deferred her own
dreams to support her children, cautions them to stay
focused on their present responsibilities.

It is through the spiritual and athletic Guapa,
then, who brings to the family dreams of a better
Future. Contrast the "dirty ol' town" with the
landscape of a green, open *futbol* field. A place of
play. A place where goals are made through talent,
practice, and ability. *Futbol-arte.* Svich's poetic

theatricality resonates for all of us who are nostalgic for the past, are frustrated by the present, and aspire for the future.

---Heather Helinsky, dramaturg

Lifegame/Life's game: Writing GUAPA
By Caridad Svich

here we sit
half seen
in the dusty bowl
of the dust bowl -
giants to some
invisible to others
surviving another day
because it is all we can do.

Some plays are like water. They flow, from a seemingly never ending river where memory, desire, old jokes, music, and good hauntings reside. *Guapa* is one of those plays.

The seeds of it stirred several years ago (2006) when I was a visiting playwright at Bennington College during a particularly bleak and unsettled winter. I was wrestling with writing itself, and its unforgiving angels and monsters, and wondered if I should keep writing at all. Guapa's voice started to come to me in prose. And so, I began a short story about a girl in a town (very loosely based on fragments of Austin, Texas and environs),walking through a scarred land full of hope. Her voice as a character, unlike other voices I'd recorded before on the page, was struck with an irrevocable plain-ness mixed with impossible yearning and a sly, pragmatic sense of humor. It was, for all intents and purposes, my first "grown-up" (as in, written after graduate school) prose piece, and the combination of being in unfamiliar, isolated surroundings in wintry Vermont, and faced with a new voice on the page kept me in the fight against the demons that sometimes torture writers when they're at a cross-roads in their writing life.

I set the prose piece aside, but that summer it whispered back to me while I was in Austin, Texas working on the premiere of my play with slaughter songs *Thrush* with Salvage Vanguard Theatre. The play is the second in my "land and country" series of plays that began with *Fugitive Pieces*, and is rife with haunted echoes of angry ballads, mournful laments, and punk-ish quartets about the plight of women and war and women in war. The troubled nature of *Thrush* as well as the difficult circumstances of its physical production: the play was being produced in an unfinished raw space with limited electrical capacity and vast acoustical challenges served as backdrop for long walks along Austin's streets, as I seeked solace from what the earth could tell me. It was on these walks that Guapa kept whispering. I listened, half-heartedly, and took occasional notes in my writing journal, but thought nothing much of it all, and let the prose stirrings be.

A year later (2007), this time on Whidbey Island in Washington at the Women's Playwrights Festival hosted by Hedgebrook along with Seattle Repertory, Guapa's voice returned, and along hers were voices of other un-named characters that demanded to be written. In the small cabin on the island, I noted a mere handful of monologues and a couple of scenes in my journal. I thought they would become part of another play I was tentatively naming *Giants*, winking slyly at one of my favorite novels Edna Ferber's *Giant* (1952) and equally favorite films (1956), which has the distinction of not only being a pretty damn good Hollywood movie, but also the last onscreen performance rendered by James Dean. Mad, sweeping, vast Texas is at the centre of *Giant*, as novel and film. Although my only connection to Texas is with my work - my plays *Fugitive Pieces*, *Thrush*, *Iphigenia….a rave fable*, *Antigone Arkhe*, and *The House of the Spirits* have been produced in Dallas, Austin, College Station and Houston – one of my most vivid memories as a young adult was traveling cross country in my parents' car from Florida to California with a seemingly endless passage through the very long state of Texas. The passage included an unlikely detour into a ghost town, where I took some of my most cherished personal photographs of abandoned "life." So, you could say that Texas has been with me in mind for a long time, and not just in my work but also in song.

One of the strongest aesthetic connections I have is to the music and storytelling of Texas popularized by singer-songwriters such as Buddy Holly, Roy Orbison, and Townes Van Zandt, among many others. Seemingly effortless, stick in your heart and mind music that with it, for me, anyway, carries also the inevitable influences of Texas swing and also the music of Spain, Mexico, and France (all at one time countries that had power over the state). Many of my own lyrics and melodies as a songwriter owe an acknowledged debt to the kinds of musical storytelling learnt from the craftsmen and women and vocalists associated with the Texas and Tex-Mex sound. I listened to country-western music a great deal as an adolescent, wrapping my tongue round the rough-hewn, beautiful, (mostly) acoustic vernacular that felt peculiar and defiant, as peculiar and defiant as *cante jondo* and flamenco, and the tremulous, operatic *boleros* sung by Spanish language pop star divas and divos.

Much, of course, has been written about and rhapsodized over, and even hammered about the volatile, strange, open, and mysterious landscape and politics of the Lone Star state. Films, songs, visual art, dance… you name it, someone's written about That Place. Although *Guapa* is set in an un-named town in the state, the varied, complex, rich history and associations that the state carries in and out of the imaginary is inextricably part of the piece. So, is that what I was thinking about when I was miles away on lovely, idyllic Whidbey Island?

The play wasn't even a play, then. In fact, I jettisoned the characters that kept whispering to me, in favour of others that took over, and so not one, but at least ten more plays were written between 2007 and 2010, before I found myself once again hearing Guapa's voice. This time it was in the most seemingly unlikely of places: the Chilean desert. It was the summer of 2010 and my play *The House of the Spirits* was receiving a pre-premiere, in my Spanish-language version, in an old salt-mining ghost town named Humberstone in a theatre from the 1800s that had been originally built for Enrico Caruso. Here in the red desert, miles and miles away from absolutely anything in an old restored opera house Guapa returned. It was as if I could see her kicking a soccer ball in the sand and dirt under a moonstruck night. Is she ghosting me? I wondered. With a laugh, I set the vision aside and carried on with my work, but a part of me thought, why is she back now? What does she want? And what has she to do with my writing life, or the game of writing itself?

My father was a professional soccer player. He was a goal-keeper for several pro teams in Argentina, Colombia, Guatemala, Mexico and Canada for about ten years (1950s to 1962). There was even a haphazard stint in Spain, so he's told me. My father's scrapbook and life before I was born, a life led in South America and partly in North America, has also been part of my upbringing. Although he didn't play once he emigrated to the US with my mom (who is Cuban), talk of soccer dominated a portion of my life, and his red leather scrapbook of press clippings mixed in with X-rays of his old sports injuries was a source, for me, of undeniable glamour and mystery. Strong, graceful, brave soccer players took the field on the television screen when I was growing up. The games were mostly broadcast on the Spanish-language TV stations, not on the main US network channels. The ecstatic holler of "Gooooooooooooooooooaaal" was a familiar refrain when I was a child, as I wrote little stories in my notebook - a life's game barely begun.

Futbol is a beautiful sport. Pages and pages have been written and sung about it in texts on globalization and economics theory, sports memoirs, reggae, punk and rock n roll songs, political manifestos, and poetry. *Guapa*, of course, is not about *futbol per se*. It is about many things, as most plays are, but mainly about the riddles and micro-shifts and little miracles that occur in life. It's an everyday play, a family play, and an aspirational story. The prism is *futbol*, Texas in the real and imaginary, syncretic, hybrid Latinidad, and being working class.

It is also a play where I re-find what started me on this strange, precarious path of a writing life in the first place: the whispered voices, the shouts and songs, the games we live, and the ones we set aside for life.

> *clouded*
> *and shorn*
> *we seek*
> *a space of forgiveness*
> *not long now*
> *is the cry*
> *not long*
> *before*
> *all may fall*
> *and yet, all good things*
> *will come.*

GUAPA a play by Caridad Svich.

Full length in two acts. Cast: 3 women (1 in her 40s-50s, 2 college age), and 2 men (both college age), all preferably mixed race Latina/o. Set: single, two-location set. Some projection & video design required. Running time: approx. 110 minutes.

Synopsis: Single-mom Roly lives in a dusty Texas town that everyone longs to escape. She's never seen anything like Guapa, a natural-born athlete with a fiery ambition to become an international soccer star. When Guapa joins Roly's family, everyone's life is turned upside down. With only one shot to reach the big leagues from the barrio, how can Guapa convince the non-believers to let go of their doubts, spread their wings and fly?

Characters: GUAPA, aspiring soccer player, US Latina, fast and quick on the field, good-hearted, fiery, and a bit dreamy too, has lived a very hard life already, college age (20s) but sometimes still seems a teenager.
ROLANDA "ROLY", Guapa's guardian, US Latina with a trace of Irish, quick-tempered, passionate, pragmatic, in her 40s-50s. [her nickname is pronounced: Role-lee]
HAKIM, Roly's ward, cousin of LEBÓN's, easygoing, slyly funny, peace-maker type, wants to travel and move ahead in life, college-age, early 20s.

LEBÓN, Roly's son, impetuous, volatile, perhaps somewhat sullen, good-hearted, college age, early 20s. [his name is pronounced like the Spanish "Ramon."]
PEPI, Roly's daughter by a different father, intelligent, perceptive, practical, college age, early 20s.
And VO: RADIO DJ, voice on the radio, unseen.

Time: The present.
Place: A "dirty" old town along many borders. Somewhere in Texas.
Setting: Low light, flat space and wildflowers growing out of nothing. Harsh back country of dust and dirt, where along the highway, wayward billboards blare paint-chipped ads for stores and sales long gone. In this place, barren lots and dried-up riverbeds are the surfaces where *futbol* pickup games are played.

Notes: All the characters in this play are to greater and lesser degrees bilingual (English-Spanish) and code switch between the languages freely as natural part of their daily idiom. Some of the characters are trilingual (English-Spanish-Quechua).
Words and phrases in brackets [ ] are not meant to be spoken, and are only provided for the actor's contextualization.
Melody to the author's original songs in the text may be obtained by contacting the author directly, or the author's lyrics may be re-set by another composer.

Part One
Prologue

*Exterior. Day. In suspended time. From Guapa's pov, we
see snapshots from dream and memory:*
*[Note: these images are seen, intercut, throughout Guapa's
spoken text.]*
*Image of a road that seems to go on endlessly is seen,
against the eerie beauty of cloud bursting. Instrumental
music is heard: open, ambient, scratchy guitar with a hint
of "rata cosmica."*
*Guapa is revealed, framed in light, as images fade in and
out, dovetailing into each other:*
*A small, simple house in the middle of a patch of dirt, dust
and wild grass,*
a lone backyard in hazy afternoon light,
an Horchata kiosk outside a local, hometown supermarket,
a barren line of abandoned railroad tracks,
a faded billboard advertising the lottery,
*a truck going down an endless road, trailing a stream of
wedding carnations in its wake,*
a rough-hewn soccer field, as if seen from above,
*a goalkeeper's net, in mid frame, as if strangely suspended
in mid air,*
*and then, a slowly, reverse angle shot of a close-up of a
soccer ball, in motion, as if propelled by an invisible force…*

GUAPA: She made herself a-crazed with longing.
She was feathers and dirt made. That was she.
A *guapa* made of dirt, feathers and *futbol*.
She walked round with her hem up,

19

boots on, and legs fresh,
Futbol running through her head
like there was a host of angels and saints
callin' out her name as she moved
'cross the flat pitch of the field: "Guapa, Guapa,
Guapa..."
She smiled.
Not that anyone could see.
No one was really lookin' [here] in this dusty earth.
To them all: it was just wildflowers
shootin' up through the cracks in the itchy grass,
plain ol' legs kickin' a *futbol* down a scraggly patch.

She lets go a cry.
"Hush," the saints say, "Not so loud.
"You don't want the whole world to hear you...
just yet."
And so, the hushed girl sings a low sound.
Low n' aching, like them all, over there by the depot,
River-crossed, land-crossed. Waiting for a day's pay.
Hungry for a dollar's wage 'til the next and next...

She waves to them,
as she runs off the dirt field,
aglow in some imagined victory, and calls out:
"*Oye, Oye*, where you working today?" [1]
They look at her, and reply with swallowed grunts
and cool *chisme* on their tongues.[2]

---

[1] Translation for Oye, oye: Hey, hey.
[2] Translation for chisme: gossip.

"That girl," they say,
"that *Guapa* with them feathers, what's she made of?
What's there sparkling under her dirty eyes?"
She's not telling.
She's waiting too,
like them all there,
Waiting to be born.

Image: On what is now a majestic soccer field, a soccer ball,
in motion, rolls and rolls…

Scene One.

Exterior. Late afternoon. In present time. A field of dirt and
dust in the middle of what feels like nowhere.

ROLY (VO): Guapa! What are you doin? It's time for
supper! … Guapa! I'm talking to you!
GUAPA: *Ya voy!*[3]

The image of the projected soccer ball becomes now a real
soccer ball that rolls on. It has been kicked from some other
part of a makeshift field. GUAPA follows in pursuit. She
executes a combo of freestyle soccer tricks with the ball,
delighting in play. A display of power and inventiveness,
punctuated by breaths, grunts and perhaps even little
whoops. After a short while…
ROLY (VO): Guapa!
GUAPA: And inside on the left,

---

[3] Translation for Ya voy: I'll be right there!

and flick and twist,
and she goes, and goes
ROLY (VO): Guapa!
GUAPA (CONT): and:

She kicks ball back to unseen area of the field. She shouts,
racing, perhaps even dancing…

GUAPA:
Goal!!
!!!

She runs away.

Scene Two.

Interior. Several minutes later. Roly's house. ROLY is
setting assorted homemade food onto the small kitchen
table. GUAPA runs in. [Note: overlapping is encouraged
in this scene, where appropriate; there should be a definite
overflowing sense of life.]

GUAPA: Oo…smells good.
ROLY: Wash up before you sit down at this table. I
don't want your *microbios* everywhere.[4]
GUAPA: Don't have *microbios*.
HAKIM *(entering from within)*: You have all kinds of
microbios.
GUAPA: Shut up, Hakim.

---

[4] Translation for microbios: microbes or germs.

HAKIM (*playful*): It's true. The other day you were out there by Fiesta Market[5] and you were sticking your hands everywhere.
GUAPA: Bullshit.
ROLY: Don't talk to your brother like that.
GUAPA: He's not my-
ROLY: You know what I mean.

Guapa goes to bathroom, unseen. [Note: In production, if simultaneity of physical locations allows, there is also the option that Guapa returns to practice soccer in the backyard here, and only goes to unseen bathroom mid-way through the scene, before she has to re-enter and join everyone for dinner.]

PEPI (*entering from within*): *Rata-peludo.*
HAKIM: What are you callin' me?
PEPI: Hakim *Rata-peludo.*
HAKIM: Where'd you get that?
PEPI: That's what they all call you at school.
HAKIM: All who?
PEPI: Your "peeps" in accounting.
HAKIM: They do?
PEPI: I hear them in the quad. Furry rat.
HAKIM: Whaat?
PEPI (*playful*): Break it down. *Rata*: rat. *Peluso*: furry.
LEBÓN (*entering from within*): School sucks.
ROLY: Don't call it "school." It's college.

---

[5] Fiesta market is a chain of US Latino supermarkets/general stores popular in Texas and especially with immigrant communities.

LEBÓN: Community college.

ROLY: What's important is WHAT you learn, not WHERE you learn it.

LEBÓN: What country are you in?

ROLY: I know what I'm saying, Lebón.

LEBÓN: Ma, if you go to an Ivy, you got entry. Free pass into the WORLD. If you go to community, you got…Mickey D's. Or Walmart.

PEPI *(To Lebón)*: That's a reductive point of view.

LEBÓN: Do the math, Pepi.

PEPI: I do. Every day.

LEBÓN: Astrophysics, eh? And where does it get you? You're still here, sis. Still stuck here in this dirty ol' town.

HAKIM *(sings refrain from The Pogues' version of "Dirty Old Town")*: "Dirty old town,

LEBÓN & HAKIM *(singing together)*: "dirty old town…"

They extend the refrain, enjoying themselves…

ROLY: …Not so loud! You give me a headache!

PEPI: [Such a] Retro nuisance!

HAKIM: It's a good song.

PEPI: Old Irish crap.

HAKIM: Hey, don't diss The Pogues, man. They're classic.

PEPI: Classic what?

LEBÓN: Punk, sis. Punk, drunk, rock n' roll.

PEPI: Irish crap to me.

ROLY: Hey! We're part Irish. Remember!

HAKIM: Really? Thought you were making that up.

ROLY: I wouldn't make something like that up. No, no. Somewhere in all the crazy love in our family, there was an Irishman or two…

LEBÓN: Members of the San Patricio Brigade. That's right.

ROLY: What are you talking about?

LEBÓN: Got this whole thing laid out. 1846: some Catholic Irish guy's somewhere in north Texas, heads down to Mexico, joins up for a while with Saint Patrick's Battalion in the Mexican-American War, and then settles down in Mexico with an Indian chick and then later he dies, and she marries this-

ROLY: Whoa. Whoa. Where are you getting all this?

LEBÓN: Google.

ROLY: Our family's not on Google.

LEBÓN: How do you know?

ROLY: Because the O'Perez's are not gonna be there.

PEPI: Why not?

ROLY: Our history hasn't been written yet.

LEBÓN: Precisely. That's what I'm doin'.

ROLY: Inventing history is not the same as writing history.

LEBÓN: Our histories get invented in the textbooks all the time. Why shouldn't we invent ours for a change?

ROLY: Because then, nobody will know anything, and it'll just be a big mess.

PEPI: Already is.

Brief moment.

HAKIM: Sometimes I dream about Ireland.

PEPI: Why?

HAKIM: Want to travel, see the world.

PEPI: Go places!

HAKIM: Absolutely.

LEBÓN: Well, it's all about money, bro. If you got it, you can go anywhere. Ireland, Scotland, Russia...

PEPI: It's not ALL about money. If you keep your GPA up, you got as good a chance to travel, and do anything as anyone else, anywhere else.

ROLY: That's right. Look at your cousin Rogelio...He went to community college. Studied hard, and found his way.

LEBÓN: But he was a genius, Ma.

ROLY: And Obama?

LEBÓN: Well... but he went to Harvard, too.

ROLY: What I'm saying is-

(as Roly is about to pick up glass of water)

LEBÓN: Don't.

ROLY: ...?

LEBÓN: Better off with tequila than water.

ROLY: What are you-?

LEBÓN: Ninety percent ground water contamination.

ROLY: It's not that bad.

LEBÓN: Yes, it is!

ROLY: Well, it wasn't on the news.

LEBÓN: You think they report everything? But if you research...

PEPI: On Google.

LEBÓN: Don't be a pest.

ROLY: *Bueno*…I'll have nothing, then. *(calling out)* Guapa! Food's getting cold.[6]

GUAPA *(from off)*: *Ya voy!*

ROLY: What's that girl doin'?

PEPI: Must be washin' up. She played a pickup game today.

HAKIM: Street game?

PEPI: One of the lots 'round here.

ROLY: Don't like her playing pickup games, *peladas* with strangers. It worries me. [7]

HAKIM: Who'd she play this time?

PEPI: Said she was gonna hang out with Chico and his crew.

LEBÓN: But Chico has factory today.

PEPI: Some other crew, then. Guapa said she was gonna kick some serious ass.

LEBÓN: Nail them in the *cojones.*[8]

PEPI: Bend it like effing Beckham.

HAKIM: Hell with Beckham. Pelé, man. Pelé was the king. Before everybody.

LEBÓN *(in Portuguese, putting on Brazilian accent, but unknowingly mis-saying the phrase)*: *Molto obrigato.*

HAKIM *(putting on Brazilian accent, with affection)*: Viva Brasil!

ROLY: Nothing but *futbol* in her head.

PEPI: *Futbol-arte.*

ROLY: Huh?

---

[6] Translation for Bueno: well.
[7] Translation for peladas: pick-up games in soccer.
[8] Translation for cojones: balls.

PEPI: That's what Guapa calls it.

LEBÓN: It's soccer.

ROLY: Well, everyone in the world calls it *futbol*.

LEBÓN: We don't.

ROLY: Because it's "un-American?"

PEPI: Guapa's real good. She could be total pro.

ROLY: Silly dream.

PEPI: Why?

ROLY: Because WHAT is she going to do with *futbol-arte*? If she were a boy...

LEBÓN: Like Beckham, eh?

ROLY: Beckham, Ronaldo, Messi[9]. Ah, that Lionel Messi has God in his feet!

HAKIM: Or Zidane.[10]

ROLY: Don't mention Zidane to me. Not after what he did in his final, international match.

LEBÓN: He was provoked.

ROLY: Head butting another player is a disgrace to the sport.

LEBÓN: That was 2006, Ma!

ROLY: It was a disgrace! After all Zidane did for *futbol*, for the world,

HAKIM: For Algeria!

PEPI: ...Well, Beckham's still hot.

LEBÓN: Pepi's in looove with some old guy.

---

[9] References to famous pro soccer players: David Beckham, Cristiano Ronaldo (current star of Real Madrid team) and Lionel Messi (current star of Barcelona's pro soccer team).
[10] Reference to Zinedine Zidane, the legendary French-Alegerian player.

PEPI: I can admire Beckham's hot-ness. Besides, he's married.

LEBÓN: And SHE's hot.

PEPI *(tickling him perhaps)*: Ooo….Posh Spice.

LEBÓN: Get off.

PEPI *(references Spice Girls hit "Wannabe", perhaps tickling him, going on…)*: Tell me what you want, what you really, really want…

LEBÓN: Don't be a pest. That's like pre-school.

ROLY *(in a reverie)*: *Futbol* is a glorious sport for men. Such rhythm and grace. It's like a ballet when they're out there on the field.

PEPI: And women too.

ROLY: But they earn WHAT? Never like the men.

PEPI: And Marta of Brazil[11]?

ROLY: Well, Marta is…

HAKIM: So, so awesome.

PEPI: Made $500,000 the year she played with the LA Sol.

ROLY: And where's the LA Sol now? Marta is a superstar – the whole world of *futbol* knows her - but she still doesn't make the same as the men.

PEPI: One day…

ROLY: Never. … Don't look at me like that. How long have women being fighting for basic equality? The day women earn the same as men at *futbol,* and EVERYTHING ELSE, then we'll have something to talk about.… Guapa!

---

[11] Women's Soccer/Football superstar Marta Vieira da Silva.

GUAPA: *(from off)* Can't a person live in peace around here?

ROLY: *(calling back)* Not when it comes to food. Come on. Plate's getting cold.

PEPI: Guapa should play pro.

HAKIM: As good as her game is…

ROLY: *Ay,* if it was gonna happen, it would've happened already.

PEPI: What about Hope Solo[12]?

ROLY: Huh?

PEPI: Hope Solo's thirty-one and she's still playing pro.

HAKIM: Best goalkeeper of all time.

LEBÓN: Totally kicked ass in the Olympics.

ROLY: Is Guapa Hope Solo? Guapa's life is a whole different story.

LEBÓN: … If Guapa's step-dad hadn't…

ROLY: Do not talk to me about him. After the mess he made of his life and Guapa's and… May he rot in prison, *cabrón desgraciado de la chingada mierda.*[13]

A moment.

HAKIM: They call me towel-head.

ROLY: What?

HAKIM: At college.

LEBÓN *(riding him)*: 'Cuz that's what you are.

HAKIM: Am not.

---

[12] Olympic US womens soccer team goalkeeper Hope Solo.

[13] Literal translation for cabron desgraciado de la chingado mierda: disgraceful asshole of the fucking shit.

LEBÓN: What are you, then, with a name like Hakim?

HAKIM (joking): Man, I'm like Shakira.

PEPI (singing softly the Shakira refrain, underscoring during the next several lines...): "Hips don't lie..."

LEBÓN: Whaaat?

HAKIM: You know, all mixed up and shit. I'm the perfect multiethnic ethnic!

LEBÓN: Straight to Bollywood, eh?

HAKIM: Slumdog of the slumdogs!

ROLY: We are not in a slum!

PEPI: That is so totally messed up. Bollywood is not even a reference for multi-ethnicity.

LEBÓN: It's a globalized no man's land, right? I can make Bollywood stand for everything.

Guapa enters.

GUAPA: Fuck everyone who thinks we're just wetbacks and freeloaders!

ROLY: No language at the table please! Not while you're in my house.

GUAPA: Want me to leave, then?

ROLY: Just sit. Let's eat in peace.

GUAPA: Yes, Roly.

ROLY: And don't call me by my name. I'm *Tia* Roly to you.

GUAPA: But you're not my real...

ROLY: We have blood...somewhere... And now that we're ALL here, we should say grace. Come on. Join hands.

They do.

ROLY (CONT): Go on, Guapa.
GUAPA: Me?
ROLY: It's your turn.
GUAPA: But I don't even…
ROLY: It's your turn.
GUAPA *(after slight moment)*: Well…uh… Thank St. Therese, the Little Flower, for protectin' me every day, and teachin' me about how beautiful the wildflowers are, and thanks to all the saints,
ROLY: And God.
GUAPA: And God… for all this food we got here, and for… this house and… for all the amazing *futbol* players on this earth,
HAKIM: And us.
GUAPA: And us. Yeah. But most of all, thanks to *futbol-arte*, cause it's the best sport ever, and one day the whole world, includin' this little town and the whole state of Texas, is gonna know it. Amen.
ALL: Amen.

They eat.

PEPI: How was the game?
GUAPA: It was all right.
HAKIM: Still workin' on your trick kick?
GUAPA: I'll nail it one of these days.
HAKIM: We can watch Marta again later.

GUAPA: Man, I've seen her trick kick on YouTube, like, a million times. But I still can't get it. She makes it look so easy. Marta of Brazil is genius.
PEPI: You can be genius. If you try.
LEBÓN: ...Did Chico say where he was goin' tonight?
GUAPA: Didn't see him. Why? You gonna meet up?
ROLY: Lebón has homework.
PEPI: And a ton of it, too.
LEBÓN: I can do homework AND meet up with Chico.
ROLY: You're not so good at the multi-tasking.
LEBÓN: What's that mean?

Roly doesn't respond.

HAKIM: Chico's a helluva left back [on the field].
GUAPA: When he wants...
ROLY: Every since I can remember... Chico's been a strange boy.
PEPI: How?
ROLY: Weird eyebrows.
PEPI *(laughing)*: What are you talkin' about?
ROLY: Like a girl.
PEPI: Ma...
ROLY: ...?
PEPI: Chico's a trans, okay?
ROLY: What?
HAKIM: Like "Boys Don't Cry."
ROLY: Chico's a *chica*? ... Well... well, all I know is his eyebrows...are very weird.
GUAPA: ...There's a *pelada* finals in Dallas.

ROLY: *Qué?*[14]
GUAPA: Comin' up soon.
PEPI: A finals?
GUAPA: Well, not a finals finals, but a really big game that can get you a chance into the national street soccer finals in DC.
ROLY: Where'd you get all-?
GUAPA: Heard. One of guys at the *pelada* today. His cousin plays for a street soccer team in Fort Worth.
HAKIM: Real organized, eh?
GUAPA: I figure if I get my game on, practice real good, at least they could see me.
ROLY: You're not getting the car, Guapa. I need the car. Lebón needs the car. And it's a broken down piece of crap car as it is.
GUAPA: Didn't say…
ROLY: If you want to go to Dallas, find somebody to take you, but I tell you right now: if you lose your job because of some *futbol* nonsense.
GUAPA: Not nonsense-
ROLY: If you lose your job, forget about staying here.
PEPI: Ma! Guapa's family.
ROLY: There have to be some rules in a house, *mi'ja*. I'm sorry, but it's the truth. I got work. *(to Pepi)* You got school; Lebón and Hakim have school and work. Guapa here doesn't go to school,
LEBÓN *(needling)*: 'Cuz she's slow.
GUAPA: Shut up!
ROLY (CONT): So, WORK is all she got.

---

14 Translation for Que: what?

GUAPA: I bag groceries.

ROLY: Is it work or is it not work? Like everyone here. You either got work or school. Or both. I'm not having *pinches vagabundos* in my house.[15]

LEBÓN: Dad was enough of a slacker shit for all of us.

ROLY: Don't talk about your father like that!

LEBÓN: But it's-

ROLY: I can talk about him like that. But not you! Neither you nor Pepi can talk about either of your fathers like that. They may have had their issues, but they're still your fathers. Show some respect.

GUAPA: …But it could be a chance for the real finals.

ROLY: *Qué?*

GUAPA: At Dallas.

ROLY: And what? That will be the last street soccer finals ever in the history of all the-?

GUAPA: The guy today said there are gonna be scouts…

HAKIM: For pro stuff?

GUAPA: Uh-huh.

ROLY: You are not going to be pro, Guapa. Put your feet on the ground. Face the world with clear eyes.

GUAPA: But the saints… speak to me.

PEPI: St. Therese, the Little Flower?

GUAPA: All of them.

LEBÓN: And what do they tell you?

GUAPA: All kinds of things.

HAKIM: Like what?

---

[15] Translation for pinche vagabundos: damn vagabonds.

GUAPA: 'Bout how mercy is granted to those who practice real hard.

HAKIM: Mercy, eh?

GUAPA: And how if you believe in somethin', no matter how crazy-shit it is, it could happen someday.

LEBÓN (*joking*): You tell the saints to bless me, then, and get me the hell out of this town.

ROLY: *No digas esas cosas!*

LEBÓN: You think anybody ever put their finger on a map, and said, Oh yeah I'd like to live there – right there, in the middle of scrub and *puro* flat-ness.[16]

ROLY (*to Guapa*): Look, even if, even if you had a saint-blessed, kind of ability,

PEPI: She does.

ROLY (CONT, *to Pepi*): Do you really think some scout from some *pinche* pro club is gonna pick someone like her?

GUAPA: What's that mean?

LEBÓN: …Means you're too peasant, that's what she means.

ROLY: Did not say-

GUAPA: Peasant?

LEBÓN: "Backward *chippy chola*."

GUAPA (*on the attack*) What the fuck?

ROLY: Hey. Hey. *Deja!*

LEBÓN: Not my words. I'm just quoting.

GUAPA: Quoting who?

LEBÓN: Racist ass-wipes that hang out by the Sip n' Dip over on MLK [Blvd].

---

[16] Translation for puro: pure.

GUAPA: I'll kick their ass.

ROLY: You are going to do nothing of-

GUAPA: They think they can stand around and say stupid shit about me, I'll show them!

ROLY: Guapa.

GUAPA: Got no right!

ROLY: Guapa!

GUAPA: If they wanna call me things, call them to my face! Let's see if they got the *huevos* to do that, racist *mierdas*! I'll fuckin' two-piece 'em! [17]

ROLY: Enough!

Roly stops Guapa from leaving.

GUAPA: Want me to just take it?

ROLY: No, but-

LEBÓN: I'LL kick their ass.

GUAPA: Let's do it, then!

ROLY: *POR FAVOR!* NOBODY is gonna kick anybody's ass around here. That's not how we do things!

LEBÓN: How is it we do things, then? We let people talk, call us whatever and swallow it all like good little nobodies that got no rights? We were here BEFORE them, Ma, waaay before, and they're still-

ROLY: Look, one day, one day ...we'll dream all the big dreams...

LEBÓN: And meanwhile, what? Head down to the border and hope for a job workin' for homeland

---

[17] Translation for huevos and mierda, respectively: eggs, shit.

security or border patrol cuz that's the only stuff that really pays?

ROLY: I never said-

LEBÓN: Or join the Army? Those are the options we got, Ma.

HAKIM: There are the oil rigs.

LEBÓN: Like I'm gonna do that shit.

HAKIM: It's money.

LEBÓN: Drill and drill until what? Ruin the planet completely? No. Won't do that.

HAKIM *(riding him, pushing his buttons)*: Eco-freak.

LEBÓN: You're the freak, man.

HAKIM: Huh?

LEBÓN: For even makin' a case for them.

HAKIM: I am not-

LEBÓN: Guapa should kick some ass. Hakim should kick some ass, too. Hell, even Pepi here should kick some ass.

PEPI: Don't you bring me into-

ROLY: Listen now: we're eating. We're here. Let's just be here. You think I never dreamed about anything in my life? I had all kinds of dreams...

PEPI *(with a caress toward her mother):* Ma...

ROLY: But if there's one thing I know: dreams alone can't carry us.

LEBÓN: What?

ROLY: Listen, one day you will all move out of this house and live your own lives...

GUAPA: ... But I play real good. I have as much right as... You know, I can ask if they can put me on double shifts between now and… that way I wouldn't technically be missing out on work.

ROLY: …We'll see.

GUAPA: I could show those scouts a thing or two. Even if I am "peasant."

A moment.

HAKIM: Food was good.

ROLY: Poor man's food, like my grandma used to say: "*La bendicion que tienen los pobres es que pueden vivir a base de arroz y frijoles!*" (translation: Bless the poor because they can live on beans and rice!)

LEBÓN (*under*): Spanish all the time…

HAKIM: Not all the time.

LEBÓN: You listenin' or aren't you?

HAKIM: More than you think.

LEBÓN: Is that right?

ROLY: At least I have two languages. Not like everyone else 'round here-

GUAPA: Wouldn't even let me speak Spanish.

PEPI: How's that?

GUAPA: When I was in school…

ROLY: That's because we live in a crazy country, where having only one language is considered a sign of superiority. … I made dessert. Who wants some?

PEPI: *Ay*, Ma, it's too much.

ROLY: Want to starve, *mi'ja*, like all the *Americanas*?

PEPI: I am American.

GUAPA: What'd you make?

ROLY: *Tres leches* with angel food cake.

PEPI (*makes gesture of Rhinoceros horns*): *Postre para rinocerontes!*

LEBÓN: Stop with the Spanish shit.

PEPI & ROLY: It's not shit!

LEBÓN: It's not even our (*in Quechua, meaning "blood", pronunciation:* **yah**·*wahr*) *yawar*.

ROLY: What?

LEBÓN: *Yawar*.

GUAPA: I'll have some cake.

ROLY: That's the spirit! A little sweetness in life! And not to brag, but the *tres leches* turned out really good this time! I used grandma's secret ingredient!

PEPI: Rum?

ROLY: How'd you-?

PEPI: *shrugs*

ROLY: Well, there's another secret ingredient, but I'm not going to tell you. You'll have to guess!

GUAPA: …What's it mean again: *yawar*?

LEBÓN: Blood.

GUAPA (*trying the word in her mouth*): *Yawar*.

PEPI: Are you still watching that guy giving Quechua lessons on YouTube?

LEBÓN: Every single day. Ever since Guapa got here… Your Ma, right? She was an Inca.

GUAPA: Didn't really know her.

LEBÓN: Got her language.

GUAPA: No. All I got is just words every once in a while…come into my brain. You know more Quechua words than I do.

LEBÓN: I bet you know them all. Deep down somewhere. And one day they'll just rise up like…

(And then he says in Quechua, "to be able to believe,"
pronunciation: ah·tee, ee·nee)

LEBÓN (CONT): *Ati iny.*

(And then he says….pronunciation: nyow·pah, yah·wahr):

LEBÓN (CONT): *Ñawpa yawar.*

(And then he translates it for her)

LEBÓN (CONT): To be able to believe in ancient blood.
PEPI: Getting good at it.
LEBÓN: 'Cuz I practice.
GUAPA: Sounds nice.
LEBÓN: And one day, I bet Quechua and all the indigenous languages are gonna rise up, and take over all the colonial crap we've bought into.
HAKIM: Haven't bought into anything.
LEBÓN: Don't even know what you're sayin', bro.
HAKIM: Live here, don't I?
LEBÓN: Live here now.
HAKIM: This town ain't ALL of Texas, man.
PEPI: We're not emblematic. That's right.
LEBÓN: Like I give a shit about that. I'm talkin' indigenous, okay?
ROLY: Don't know where you're getting all this nostalgia.
LEBÓN: It's not-

ROLY: Your Dad was not an Inca, Lebón. Never in his sorry life did he speak a word of Quechua.

LEBÓN: Wasn't talking about my Dad. Why does everything I do have to be about my Dad? I'm not my Dad, okay? Not remotely like him! You're always on me about how I look like him and stuff.

ROLY *(with affection)*: Who are you gonna look like?

LEBÓN (CONT): I'm talking about being Indian, right? About owning up to the fact that that's what we have inside of us, that that's the blood we have to acknowledge, and it's the blood that people keep asking us to push away.

PEPI: Dis-identify.

LEBÓN: Exactly. When there's this whole MOVEMENT of people rising up, claiming who we-

ROLY: Listen, listen, I went through all that pre-Columbian, back to Aztlán phase way back when-

PEPI: Aztlán is not the same as-

ROLY: I know, I know, but you know what, I gotta tell you: Quechua, Aymara, Guarani, Mayan… all those languages are hard. And you can't keep them up!

LEBÓN: Cuz nobody wants to speak them round here.

ROLY: You wanna re-claim them?

LEBÓN: It's our right.

HAKIM: Barrios and blood, man. Barrios and blood!

HAKIM and LEBÓN share a gesture of bonding.

HAKIM & LEBÓN: And the blood in the barrios gonna cut!

ROLY: Look, I've gone through years of barrios and blood and six hundred dead in one city and twenty hundred dead in another, m*ucha lengua y sangre*, and blood and more blood, *y qué*? You're dreaming of *la reconquista. Que se joda la reconquista!*

LEBÓN: Cousin Hakim's a towel-head cuz they wanna say so. I don't belong cuz people assume I was born on the other side of some fence. Pepi's so smart people don't wanna believe she really earns all her good grades; And Guapa here is what? Nothing?

GUAPA: Shut up.

LEBÓN: That's what they want you to be, right? Just be quiet Guapa. Don't act up, own up, do anything. Just be quiet Guapa eating her *tres leches* cuz she's got nothing else.

ROLY: I didn't say –

LEBÓN: Does nothing to be quiet. Guapa's Inca blood, Hakim's Spanish-Arab blood, Pepi's Dad's blood, my Dad's blood, your Irish-Mexican-Indian blood

ROLY: Ours, too.

LEBÓN: ALL THAT, all of it, has to be acknowledged, even in this town in the middle of nowhere where all we got is more and more flat-ness and abandoned railroad tracks from some time way back, when the Great Northern Railroad was supposed to come through here and make something happen. Our blood, which has been in this land, and through this land, and through all our lands, even further down south than anyone even thinks about, HAS to be acknowledged, be it through *futbol* or astrophysics or accounting or kicking ass, or really doing something: making some kind of sign.

ROLY: And when you make your sign, what, *mi'jo*?

LEBÓN: Got no idea.

ROLY: Lebón, I'm talking to you.

Lebón walks away.

ROLY: LEBÓN!

Lebón exits. SFX: The sound of a screen door slamming. Brief moment.

HAKIM: He just needs to walk it off.

A moment.

ROLY: You win today?

GUAPA: Yeah.

PEPI: Goal?

GUAPA: Straight into the net.

Scene Three

Exterior. Later the same evening. Roly's house. Roly sings in Spanish, as she cleans up after dinner. She is trying very hard not to be upset. [Notes: The song has a bright, gently rolling, allegro tempo. This should not be played as Roly performing for the audience, but rather as a moment in

Roly's everyday life. If necessary, the song may trail off at the asterisked line.]

"Lluvia/Rain"

ROLY: *Lluvia lenta,*
Fría, bella,
Que dices, mi lluvia
Cuando caes sobre el mar?

Lluvia lenta,
Sol de estrella,
Cierra tus ojos
En mis labios sin cesar.

Que linda, mi lluvia
Que lindo andar.
Delicia de arena,
Delicia de estar,
Aquí en tus brazos
Aquí en tu mar...
De miel y sonrisa
Y fiel libertad.[18]

---

[18] Slow rain/Cold, beautiful/What say you, my rain/As you fall upon the sea?/Slow rain/Sun's star of plenty/Rest your eyes/On my aching lips/So pretty, my rain/So pretty to roam/In sand's caress/In endless foam/Here in your arms/Here in your sea/Of honey and smiles/And true liberty.

Roly continues humming, as lights shift to backyard of Roly's house. Pepi is seated, reading from a e-textbook. Guapa dribbles an old soccer ball.

GUAPA: She's really into it.

PEPI: When she cleans…

GUAPA: More than usual.

PEPI: Never seen Lebón like that.

GUAPA: He was super mad.

PEPI: All that anger…it's not good.

GUAPA: …Saints don't mind.

PEPI: They talk to you about him?

GUAPA *(playful)*: Sometimes.

PEPI: He's just like Ma.

GUAPA: Temper.

PEPI: Yeah.

ROLY *(from Off is heard, chorus[19])*:

Aquí en tus brazos,

Aquí en tu mar…

GUAPA *(simultaneous)*: Go, Tia!

PEPI *(simultaneous)*: Go, Ma!

ROLY *(from Off)*: Focus on your studying!

PEPI: Those cleats fit okay?

GUAPA: They're all right.

PEPI: Are you sure?

GUAPA: Wadded up some newspaper, [and] stuffed it into the toes part so they'll fit.

PEPI: Like Marta of Brazil, eh?

---

[19] If part of the house is visible in the set, then Roly may be seen cleaning, in and out of rooms.

GUAPA: I'll never be like her.

PEPI: So, you'll be your own superstar. Don't the saints tell you?

GUAPA: *shrugs*.

PEPI: Not even Saint Thérèse, the little flower?

GUAPA: I walk round with her *estampita* in my pocket, so she'll protect me, but every time I look at her face, and think about everything she got to do in her life, all I can think about is how far behind I am in everything. ... I shoulda been playing in a real team by now, not kicking about in *peladas* here and there. *(tries prep for a trick kick, but misses)* These cleats are killing me. *(takes them off)*

PEPI: Want a smoke?

GUAPA: *Tia's* gonna catch you.

PEPI: Ma's cleaning. Come on. Have a cig.

GUAPA: Thought you were studying.

PEPI: Break time. *(refers to cigarettes)*: They're mint.

GUAPA *(tempted for a moment, but then...)*: You go ahead. I'm in trainin'.

Pepi lights up. A moment.

PEPI: Ma used to smoke. When I was little, my Dad and her would light the fuck up!

GUAPA: No smoking now, though.

PEPI: It's better for her. For all of us. Lebón's dad, though, was a total nightmare.

GUAPA: Yeah?

PEPI: The thing is, I think she really, really loved him. Like, love-of-my-life kind of love.

GUAPA: Think that's why Lebón is so-
PEPI: No. Lebón's just flunking out.
GUAPA: Does Roly-?
PEPI: No. And don't tell her! Cause she wants Lebón to… Guapa, you can't tell her. Cause if she finds out, she's gonna-
GUAPA: I swear.

Pepi looks back at her e-textbook.

GUAPA (CONT): Break over?
PEPI: Just need to study.
GUAPA: Test?
PEPI: Tomorrow.
GUAPA: You'll do fine.
PEPI: How do you know?
GUAPA: The saints come down and tell me. *(in Quechua) Yawar saywa. (translation: blood border, pronunciation: **yah**-wahr, **sai**-wah)*
PEPI: They speak Quechua now?
GUAPA: The saints speak everything, all the languages of the world.
PEPI: What's it-?
GUAPA: Don't know. Just words come into me. … Hey. Why's Lebón flunking out?
PEPI: Shh.
GUAPA *(whispers)*: Why?
PEPI: Cause of World History.
GUAPA *(whispers)*: Is Hakim flunking out, too?
PEPI: No. Why would he-?
GUAPA: Cause he's always-

PEPI: Listen, Hakim may not look it, but he's super focused.

GUAPA: And you're gonna be a rock star. Ladies and gentleman, *the* NEXT Latina astronaut is...

PEPI: Pepi O'Perez!

GUAPA: ...You gotta change your name. Like, big time.

PEPI: ... Who was the first Latina astronaut?

GUAPA: Ellen Ochoa. She was in space in 1993, '94, '99 and 2002.

PEPI: How'd you-?

GUAPA: I know some things. Just cuz I was shit at school-

PEPI: I didn't say-

GUAPA: I was.

PEPI: Could go back.

GUAPA: Nah. I can't remember stuff. Like homework and... I'm no good at it.

PEPI: Remembered Ellen Ochoa.

GUAPA: It was on the net.

PEPI: Freaky-ass thing to remember.

GUAPA: I am NOT going back to school.

PEPI: Just *futbol*, eh?

GUAPA: *Futbol-arte.*

PEPI: So, you gonna get Chico to take you to the big game?

GUAPA: Chico's an ass.

PEPI: What?

GUAPA: Doesn't really see me. The way the others...

PEPI: What others?

GUAPA: *shrugs.*

PEPI: Guapa! Come on.

GUAPA: ...Land crossers over by the depot.

PEPI: What are you doin' over by...? Those men are lookin' for work.

GUAPA: We just talk. About where they're from. And how long they've been waiting for work. And how there's no work most days, and then for one or two days there's this mad rush, and they gotta make their money fast, or it's gonna go away. And they look at me, and ask me where the hell my cleats are, and I tell them, "I don't need to wear cleats all the time. Sometimes it's just great to let my toes breathe and wiggle."

PEPI: That's all you talk about with those men?

GUAPA: THOSE men have names.

PEPI: Gotta watch out. Don't wanna end up like what happened with that girl and your step dad.

GUAPA: Don't want to hear about my step-dad, okay?

PEPI: Just-

GUAPA: Don't know shit 'bout what went down.

PEPI: Know enough.

GUAPA: That right?

PEPI: Ma said-

GUAPA: Like *Tia* Roly knows anythin'.

PEPI: ... Just sayin' you gotta be careful 'bout...

GUAPA: Shut up!

A moment.

PEPI: Sorry.

GUAPA: Just wanna practice, all right?

Guapa focuses intently on practicing futbol maneuvers.
Pepi watches her. After a moment…

GUAPA: I so need to get my game on.

Guapa keeps practicing.

PEPI: If you're going to go to Dallas for the game, I'll
see if I can get someone from college to take you, if
Chico won't.
GUAPA: Can't go, if my game's no good.
PEPI: You practice every day.
GUAPA: Yeah, but I gotta focus. Like, big-time.
PEPI: So the scouts can-
GUAPA: The scouts and everybody else. Why the hell
do you think I play all the time? Love the game, love
it more than anythin', but hell yeah, I want people to
see me. Man, I got this whole book-movie in my head
'bout my life that I wanna show the world.
PEPI: Book-movie?
GUAPA: Yeah.
PEPI: Tell me.
GUAPA: Like you care.
PEPI: Guapa.
GUAPA: *keeps practicing.*
PEPI: Said I was sorry.
GUAPA: *keeps practicing.*
PEPI: Look, the day you came here, what'd I say?
GUAPA: *keeps practicing.*

PEPI: Sisters. Right?

GUAPA: …

PEPI: Tell me.

GUAPA: Think it silly.

PEPI: won't.

GUAPA: … Well, in this book-movie I got in my head…

PEPI: Yeah?

GUAPA: I see a huge party, like the *quinceanera* I never had,

PEPI: Wish I hadn't had one.

GUAPA: And I'm wearing a kick-ass poufy dress, that I'd never ever wear, and it's all girly pink and I got roses in my hair,

PEPI: Super girly.

GUAPA: And there are balloons, and cherub boys all naked with silver eye-shadow on

PEPI: Total glam.

GUAPA: Yeah. It's like a pixie dust *quince* and it's also a little Goth, but everybody's into it, you know, everybody's into my party, and there are *futbol* banners everywhere mixed in with the pixie dust and glitter, and all the great players are there from all over- Barcelona and Madrid, Brazil and South Africa, Mexico and Argentina – and all the saints are there, too. Saint Therese, the Little Flower, is holdin' a soccer ball and smilin' at me, and the land-crossers are dressed up real nice and are askin' the DJ to throw some old songs into the mix – and all the girls are real trad, but in a cool way, and the boys are all angel-like and smooth with no cuts or scars or anything – no suffering on their bodies – on anyone's at this party – and everybody can see us for who we really are – the racist ass-wipes on MLK, the pro scouts, everybody. And we all – all the girls, even the ones who aren't that girly, take the boys out for a spin,

PEPI: Yeah?

GUAPA: Hell yeah. While the saints look on and give us a kinda blessin' –

Cuz it's like we're under some spell – like outta that movie "Black Swan," but without all the bi-polar freak-out stuff and messed up shit about women havin' to die because they have power – and it's like magic, the real kind, y'know? cuz everybody can touch us, and no one's scared.

PEPI: I'd like to go to that party.

GUAPA: Sometimes when I'm playin', when I'm just kickin' the ball about, I think one day the swan feathers I think I got inside me gonna sparkle so much like crazy Party Town glitter, I'm gonna do a Mardi Gras voodoo incantation, and stir up a party that's gonna take me somewhere else.

PEPI: Outta Texas?

GUAPA: Just go.

Roly walks in with a cup of coffee in hand.

ROLY: And where is it you gonna go?

GUAPA: …Nowhere.

PEPI *(to Roly)*: Finished up?

ROLY: It's all sparkling.

PEPI: Don't know why you have to clean all the time. You clean enough at work.
ROLY: Leave me to my craziness. In my house, you can eat off the floor.
PEPI: Why would anyone want to do that?
GUAPA: Made coffee?
ROLY: There's a little bit left at the bottom of the *cafetera*. But if you want more, you'll need to put some more water in the-
GUAPA: I'm on it!

Guapa runs into house to get coffee. A moment.

ROLY: Guapa and her coffee.
PEPI: Loves it.
ROLY: Caffeine and *futbol* girl. Some combination... Studying?
PEPI: Got a test.
ROLY: I like books.
PEPI: Hmm?
ROLY: The feel of them.
PEPI *(with irony)*: E-books are the now.
ROLY: Scroll with your finger? You can't even smell the pages!
PEPI: Who wants to do that?
ROLY: It's nice to smell the parchment and the history on the pages. Not all books smell the same. ... Think I'm *loca*?
PEPI: You like books.
ROLY: I. Like. Books.
PEPI: Never see you reading them.

ROLY: My eyes…they're not so good anymore.

PEPI: Wear glasses.

ROLY: How a woman looks is important.

PEPI: *laughs*

ROLY: Why is it a crime for a woman to want to present herself to the world and to her loved ones the BEST way she can?

PEPI: Got nothing to do with wearing glasses.

ROLY: … *Oye*, what's that smell?

PEPI: Huh?

ROLY: Like mint.

PEPI: Someone must be cooking.

ROLY: Cooking awfully close. … You know, if you're going to smoke, you should at least give me one.

PEPI: I wasn't-

ROLY: One smoke every once in a while isn't such a bad thing. It's when it becomes a habit…

PEPI: [sound] Just like grandma.

ROLY: Everyday I'm getting more like her. Singing old songs, cleaning…

PEPI: Miss her.

ROLY: … So many stars. Is that Orion?

PEPI: Yeah.

ROLY: When you were little, your dad and I would count the stars and wait for you to fall asleep. We'd sing: Pepi's in Orion. Pepi's in Orion.

PEPI: Why?

ROLY: We liked the way it sounded.

PEPI *(singing the improvised tune as well)*: Pepi's in Orion. Pepi's in Orion.

ROLY: That's right. Little did we know you'd end up wanting to study the stars one day.

PEPI: …Could call him.

ROLY: Your dad and I are no good for each other.

PEPI: I know, but-

ROLY: Me and men, *mi'ja,* we do not have a good track record. Listen, it's not something I'm proud of. Believe me, I thought it would work out with your dad but-

PEPI: Then, call him.

ROLY: Look, one day when you have your own family… you'll understand.

PEPI: Don't want one.

ROLY: *Pepi la Independiente?*

PEPI: That's right. … Hakim should be home by now.

ROLY: Took the late, late shift.

PEPI: Again? Ma, he can't do the late, late shift at the diner all the time with all the stuff he's got at college. He's gonna fall behind.

ROLY: Said he wanted to. They pay him more.

PEPI: Lebón could do it.

ROLY: Don't know where that boy…

PEPI: Hmm?

ROLY: Called the factory. He's not there.

PEPI: Where's he, then?

ROLY: …He's a grown man. I can't take care of him forever.

PEPI: But Ma, what if he-?

ROLY *(puts out cigarette)*: Worry about yourself. Let me worry about Lebón.

PEPI: What if something happened to him?

ROLY: Is it the first time he cuts off from work?

PEPI: No, but-

ROLY: Listen, if he wants to run around and ruin his life, let him learn his lesson.

PEPI: How can you say that?

GUAPA *(entering)*: What's going on?

ROLY*(continuing, to Pepi)*: Some people need to fall and fall hard so they can learn how to rise up in the world. Maybe Lebón is one of those people. And some people – like Hakim and you – they just rise and rise because that's their destiny.

GUAPA: What do you mean?

ROLY: Guapa, you got work in the morning. And you, *mi'ja*, you got your classes. Leave everything else to me.

PEPI: But Ma!

Roly goes back to the house. After brief moment, SFX: a bedroom door is heard slamming.

PEPI (CONT): WHAT is wrong with her?

GUAPA: What are you talking about?

PEPI: Lebón's missing.

GUAPA: Huh?

PEPI: Said she called work and that he's not there.

GUAPA: Probably hangin' out, taggin' and shit.

PEPI: Supposed to be at work. He's this close from being fired.

GUAPA: Since when?

PEPI: Do you just walk around thinking about *futbol* all the time? They've already given him two warnings at work. Third warning, and he's out.

GUAPA: Serious.

PEPI: Yeah, yeah, that IS serious, and if he flunks out of school AND gets fired, what the hell are we gonna do? Ma doesn't make enough cleaning at that stupid mall. And every day there are less and less jobs. And the jobs that ARE out there are *pinche* part-time jobs, so you basically have to have five part-time jobs just to make like you have one. So, what's Lebón gonna do? Go to Afghanistan or wherever the hell our government decides to go into next? Come back like that kid over on Main who's all PTSD and shit? And meanwhile I've got a stupid psych test tomorrow. And Hakim's working late-late shift, which means he's gonna be all sleepy-ass at school, and I'm gonna have to buy him a triple espresso latte or something over at The Bean, when my credit card is already at max. I mean, I can't put one more thing on it or they're gonna take it away from me, and I need that card, right? I fucking need it. Cuz without credit, I'm screwed. And Ma and you got work in the morning, and I have term paper due in my astronomy class and...

Pepi is near tears.

GUAPA: Want me to take the test?

PEPI: What?

GUAPA: Go to class, take the psych test...

PEPI: Are you OUT of your fucking-?

58

GUAPA: Just trying to-

PEPI: Guapa, you can't just CHEAT for me on a test-

GUAPA: I'm good at psych. Just people stuff. Like *futbol*, right?

PEPI: *Futbol, futbol, futbol*…it's all about YOU all the time, but we got a whole lotta shit going on, right? I got a whole lotta mess of obligations, and Lebón flunking out and getting his ass fired, and it'll ALL be on me, cause Ma will just Lebón slide. Oh, she says she won't. But I've seen it happen over and over, even before you and Hakim got here…even when we were kids ad he'd get into some fight in the playground or something, she would let him get away with it while I had to sit there and be perfect all the time and cover for any of his stupid shit. I'm always the one having to make nice on everything. Well, I am not making nice anymore! I will find out exactly where Lebón's hangin' out and I will give him a piece of my mind and then some… You'll see.

PEPI walks away.

GUAPA: Pepi? … You can't go lookin' for Lebón all by yourself.

Pepi exits. After brief moment, Guapa runs out, following her.

Scene Four

Interior. Early morning. Kitchen. Roly's house. Hakim walks in, from working the late-late shift. He grabs a beer from the icebox, drinks.

ROLY *(walks in from area within)*: Gonna drink before class?

HAKIM: Just a beer.

ROLY: One beer and then two beers and then you're going to college drunk.

HAKIM: Wouldn't be the only one.

ROLY: I don't care what other people do. I care what you do, what example you set.

HAKIM: You all right? … You're all zombie.

ROLY: Take a shower. You're gonna be late.

HAKIM: Hey, would you tell Pepi I need her spreadsheets from last term for the math class?

ROLY: What do you need HER spreadsheets for?

HAKIM: The lazy-ass prof has the exact same syllabus from last term. Thought I'd get a leg up.

ROLY: Well, she's not here.

HAKIM: …?

ROLY: Pepi's out.

HAKIM: All night?

ROLY: Don't wanna talk about it. Go on. Freshen up. You stink like an animal.

HAKIM *(playful)*: I am an animal! Roar! Roar!

ROLY: You're a grown man, for heaven's sake.

HAKIM: Just playing.

ROLY: Everybody wants to play all the time. As if you were still children.
HAKIM: Guapa still sleeping?
ROLY: *Qué?*
HAKIM: She's not out in the yard. She's usually practicing by now.
ROLY: She's out.
HAKIM: Both of them? They go on a double date?
ROLY: What did I say? Don't want to talk about it.

Hakim goes within. A moment. Roly is at a loss. Disoriented.

ROLY *(to herself)*: *Donde esta ese hijo mio? Donde estan estos hijos mios?*[20]

She rests her head on the table. She dreams.

A burst of sound and music, a revved-up hip-hop loop of "Pepi's in Orion" is heard as we see a projection of a graffiti of "Yaku" on the wall of the old kindergarten and through it in a burst of energy, Guapa, Pepi and Lebon. He's tagging. Pepi is revving him on. Guapa is perched atop what appears to be the roof of the kindergarten (but in stage reality, could be the kitchen countertop). They are moving and speaking (although we can't hear them) and in a free, ecstatic moment in their lives.

---

[20] Translation: Where s that son of mine? Where is he?

And in a flash of light, they are gone, as Roly stops dreaming.

She reorients herself and begins to dutifully go through morning routine, as best she can. She prepares coffee, and turns on a small portable radio. The radio DJ blares, in Spanish:

RADIO DJ (VO): *Este es el sol de la mañana en EL SOL, tu estación de estaciones, "La Favorita," aquí en radio dos, dos, punto cinco, FM: EL SOL.*[21]

On the radio: a bright four-note tune plays, the station's signature.

RADIO DJ (CONT): *Y ahora, seguimos con la ultima noticia: Seis muertos se reportan en la zona sureste de la region; los cuerpos de dos niños, tres adultos, y un infante se encontraron acribillados a balazos temprano esta mañana...*[22]

Roly immediately turns off the radio.

ROLY *(to herself)*: Nothing but death and murder...Families split to pieces...

---

[21] Translation: This is your morning sun on THE SUN, your station of stations, "Your Favorite," here on radio two, two, point five, FM: THE SUN.
[22] Translation: And now we continue with breaking news: Six deaths have been reported in the southeastern region of the city: the bodies of two children, three adults, and one infant were found shattered by bullets early this morning....

She makes the sign of the cross, and pours herself a cup of coffee. Hakim walks in, from within. He is dressed in casual clothes: jeans, light shirt, sneakers. He has backpack slung over his shoulder. He sets it down.

HAKIM: Mmm… coffee.

He pours herself a cup, drinks.

ROLY: Is that what you're wearing?
HAKIM: Uh-huh.
ROLY: Eat something. There are some *bolillos* in the cupboard.
HAKIM: Bread, bread and more bread.
ROLY: What's wrong with bread? It was good enough for Jesus…
HAKIM: I'm not Catholic.
ROLY: *Y eso?*
HAKIM: I wanna explore other religions.
ROLY: You don't choose religion. It chooses you.
HAKIM: That what your priest say?
ROLY: A spiritual life… is key to everything.
HAKIM: Like Guapa's saints.
ROLY: Guapa's a little mixed up about things. But that's okay.
HAKIM: Because she's *guapa.*
ROLY: How she ever got that name…
HAKIM: I can see it. Like, when she was born, someone holding her in her arms and thinking: yeah, Guapa… Beautiful.
ROLY: Beautiful, eh?

HAKIM: Absolutely.

ROLY: Listen, you think about religion, but don't get into that Pentecostal stuff. They're strange people.

HAKIM: It's a religion, like anything else.

ROLY: Snakes and speaking in tongues. Don't like it.

HAKIM: *laughs.*

ROLY: Think I'm joking?

HAKIM: It isn't ALL like that.

ROLY: Lebón's dad's family was old skool Pentecostal. I know ALL about it.

HAKIM: Lebón's dad was a meth-head.

ROLY: Is that what Lebón's been-?

HAKIM: Well, he…

ROLY (CONT): Lebón's dad was a pot-head and a drunk. If he'd been a meth-head, he would've been dead already.…

HAKIM: …You should tell-

ROLY: Lebón doesn't listen. Sometimes I think Lebón doesn't want to be like his dad so much [that] he'll end up being just like him.

LEBÓN, anxious, wired, walks in, carrying Guapa in his arms. He is followed by Pepi.

LEBÓN: I told her to let up. But she wouldn't…

ROLY: *Pero qué paso? (going to her) Guapa? Guapa?*

PEPI: We were just standing there-

ROLY: Where?

PEPI: Old kindergarten.

ROLY: Doing what?

LEBÓN: Had a couple of beers.

ROLY: Getting drunk? Just like your father.

LEBÓN: Wasn't like that. Ma…

PEPI: Guapa leapt into the air.

LEBÓN: And she fell. She just fell off the roof.

HAKIM: *Gets mobile from his backpack.*

PEPI: Like, in a split second.

ROLY *(CONT, to Lebón, perhaps with a blow or two)*: What did you do? What did you do?

LEBÓN: I didn't-

ROLY: What did you do?

LEBÓN: Christ, Ma. I didn't do anything. She just fell. That's all.

ROLY *(to Guapa, as if in prayer)*: *Vamos. Vamos. Levanta ese espíritu.*

HAKIM *(on mobile)*: … Yes? This is an emergency. There's a… She's not moving. I don't know. She fell. My sister. Well…Not really, but… Look, we need an ambulance. Yes. … 421 Pine. … Yellow house. At the intersection of Ranch and Pine.

The sound of sirens, as lights fade.

Part Two
Second Prologue

Exterior. Day. In suspended time. From Guapa's pov.
[Note: the images are intercut along with the spoken text.]
Image of railroad tracks, going on for what feels like
forever, edged by rough grass. Instrumental music
underscore: spare, achingly sublime guitar, on the far edge
of twang. Dreamy, spare sound.

Guapa is revealed, framed in light, as images flash in and
out: slightly blurry, fragmented, interrupted in memory's
track:
Close-up of graffiti on the wall of the abandoned
kindergarten, reading YAKU, in bold reds and green and
yellows;
Exterior façade of the abandoned kindergarten, its vacant
parking lot overrun by weeds;
A rusted red bicycle, one of its wheels busted, leaning
against the kindergarten wall, forgotten;
Across the street, on the wall of an auto body shop, the face
of Saint Thérèse, the little flower, is seen, painted as part of
an unfinished mural – she is drawn to look a bit, oddly
enough, like movie icon Audrey Hepburn;
Dry patches of earth and houses lying low against the
horizon;
Empty beer cans, fruit rinds and sparkly gift wrap paper
nestled on the side of the road- as if an odd, impromptu
makeshift shrine;
White candles of the saints in long tall clear glasses stacked
on a wooden shelf at the local supermarket: St Martin of

Porres, St Lazarus, The Virgin of Guadalupe, The
Guardian Angel;
A pick-up truck carrying a bed of feathers: Not a feather
bed, but rather an impossible amount of feathers stacked
high one atop the other in shades of white, ivory, and
occasional, startling peacock blue;
A shot of the roof of the abandoned kindergarten and a
frayed, teetering metal ledge.
And then the image of the ledge bleeds into a strange
shower of reds, greens and yellows, as if the YAKU tag
were spilling is colors over the edge of the roof…

GUAPA: I have the faces of the saints in my hands[23]
As I'm wheeled through the hallway,
And try to forget where I live.
The hospital is strange, cold.
I like looking at the faces of the saints.
They look serene.
Ocean faces, I call them. I look at them and dream.
I pretend I'm Saint Thérèse, the little flower,
And try to make my face just like hers.
I figure if I make my face like hers I'll be beautiful too
And not just guapa
Cuz anybody can be a guapa;
Even guapas who aren't really guapas can be guapa.

But beautiful is a whole different thing.
Beautiful sings. Beautiful dreams.

---

[23] Reference to "estampitas"/saint cards usually sold in
Catholic/religious goods shops.

Beautiful like the movies
And the faces of the star-angels on the screen.
Like Audrey Hepburn. She was beautiful.
I haven't seen any of her movies
But they have her picture on the handbags
That Marisela sells over on 19th.
All these handbags with Audrey Hepburn's face.
So delicate and refined. Not a hint of *guapa*.

I'd like to be like Audrey Hepburn
Or Saint Thérèse, the little flower.
But I don't know how to make my face like that.
My face is land. Not ocean.
Even the wings I was born with,
The harsh wings that stuck in my back,
had dirt in them, from the land.

I see the word *Yaku* spray-painted on the wall of the
old kindergarten.
Lebón put it there.
The word shines blue, red and neon yellow.
It sings of water and rain.
It dreams me in Quechua; it dreams me with its
sound.

I want to kick a blazing star in that *Yaku* sky.
I want to fill it with *yawar*
And the blood of all the ancients
That speak to me in tongues like the saints do at
night.

The sky turns.
The hospital light burns.
I dream of a *pelada* somewhere far away,
And a crowd chantin' *Guapa, Guapa, Guapa...*

I wish I was the sea. So people could dream me.
So other *guapas* walking round could dream of me
As they walked around with their handbags.

Lights shift.

Scene Five

Interior. Late afternoon. Roly's house. In present time.
LEBÓN is seated, fidgeting, anxious. Hakim is standing.

HAKIM: So fulla shit.
LEBÓN: Didn't do anything.
HAKIM: Standin' on the roof of the old kindergarten taggin' some shit, like you were still in middle school, man.
LEBÓN: Wasn't shit.
HAKIM: What was it, then? What was so important you had to cut off from work?
LEBÓN: I put *Yaku* up there.
HAKIM: …?
LEBÓN: *Yaku.* Means "water" in Quechua.
HAKIM: Yeah, well, we don't speak Quechua around here, man.
LEBÓN: Water belongs to the earth.

HAKIM: Don't give me your eco-freak, pacifist bullshit.

LEBÓN: Eco-freak?

HAKIM: You were drunk, bro. Drunk as a kite playing fast and loose with your time.

LEBÓN: It's "high."

HAKIM: Huh?

LEBÓN: The expression is "high as a kite."

HAKIM: Like I give a fuck.

LEBÓN: Pepi was being as fast n loose as I was. Yeah. She come round, Guapa come round lookin' for me, Pepi was ready to chew my ass, and, man, we ended up revvin' each other. I was taggin'. They were kickin' cans. I had *Yaku* on the entire wall. And they were all: "Come on. Let's just jump the roof, and really show 'em what kinda sky we wanna make!" And we were all stompin', and full of *yawar*, man, like, deep down past and through everythin', cuz this was our time, and we were all rage, fury and drunk spit, yeah, and it was beautiful, man.

HAKIM: Is that right?

LEBÓN: And Pepi was shoutin' bout somethin' bout the stars, and Guapa was shoutin' somethin' bout some book-movie in her head, and I was taggin' like I had some kinda fire in me from some ancient time that was gonna clean all the dirty water in this town and all over Texas and give us all a brand new start, and that's when Guapa leapt into the air like she was Marta of Brazil and we all just-

HAKIM: Let her mess herself up-

LEBÓN: Were you there? Right. So you don't know what went down.

HAKIM: Don't matter WHAT went down: Guapa wanted to do whatever, she's the one that's in hospital, she's the one we don't know WHAT's going on. You were supposed to be at work.

LEBÓN: Poor man's pride.

HAKIM: What?

LEBÓN: Always gonna be down on the totem pole, bottom feeding, while the rest of the capitalist *pendejos* live off OUR blood and sweat.

HAKIM: Don't give me "the masses," man. Don't give me your neo-Marxist bullshit.

LEBÓN: It's not bullshit. You wanna believe that work is work, but who do we work FOR? We go somewhere - hot, dirty, clean whatever - we punch in eight, ten hours, and make product-

HAKIM: I work in a diner-

LEBÓN: Talkin' grand scheme, bro. We make product that someone else somewhere else buys, and then it's the product itself that ends up buying us,

HAKIM: We're epistemologically exploited. I know.

LEBÓN: But what do YOU do about it?

HAKIM: More than you.

LEBÓN: Don't give me that horseshit. The system says, "hey, keep working, asshole, cause we gotta keep the system going;" And you do it, you buy in-

HAKIM: I don't buy into anythin'.

LEBÓN (CONT): And come retirement, man, you'll be crap living paycheck to paycheck, saving *pinche* here and *pinche* there just to survive. And you wanna talk WORK like its somethin' that gives us pride. Man, I make fuckin' boxes. That's what I do in there. Cut my hands up to ship farm stuff out to God knows where, cuz we'll never see it. So yeah, I put YAKU up on that wall, cuz someone looks at it, it might make them QUESTION. But you don't get that, cuz you're all system, bro.

HAKIM: Just better pray Guapa is okay and that your little righteous stunt ain't screwed her up for life.

LEBÓN: She just slipped. Wasn't even all that high off the ground. Hell, I've jumped off that roof plenty of times.

HAKIM: If you hadn't been there...

LEBÓN: Don't lay the guilt trip on me. Don't fuckin lay it. Okay?

HAKIM: Talk and talk, cause you got your Mama supportin your ass.

LEBÓN: More like she's supportin YOUR ass.

HAKIM: Is that right?

LEBÓN: Like what you doin here, anyway? You and Guapa... Come here, eat our food, use our electric-

HAKIM: You have no idea what you're talkin about.

LEBÓN: Me and Ma get on fine. Me and Ma and Pepi get on just GREAT 'til you come ridin' into this sick-ass sunset with your "I'm your cousin I need somewhere to go" story,

HAKIM: That's NOT how it was.

LEBÓN: Forget already?

HAKIM: Came here cuz I had to, all right?

LEBÓN: Yeah yeah...Stuff back home...same ol', same ol'...

HAKIM: Man, you don't know anything 'bout anything. Think I wanted to come here? Think I like having to show up on *Tia*'s doorstep like a *mendigo*?

LEBÓN: Had my own room, man.

HAKIM: Want me to sleep on the couch? That make things all better?

LEBÓN: Have to put up with your smelly ass.

HAKIM: My ass? What about yours? You're the one fartin' all night.

LEBÓN: What?

HAKIM: Snore and fart like a fuckin' zoo parade. Think I like sleepin' next to that? I had my own room, too, back home. But man, that shit was broke. Completely broke down, like you got no idea. And no, I don't talk about, cuz it's my shit, right? My shit that got nothin' to do with you. But hey, I'm not gonna burden. Cuz that's not what I do. I deal with my own shit the way I have to. But I'm telling you, and this is fact, man, this ain't no Wikipedia bullshit, if it wasn't for *Tia* Roly – I'd be out on the street. Just like Guapa was.

LEBÓN: Do what you do.

HAKIM: Such a fucking ass.

LEBÓN: Blame Lebón for everything.

HAKIM: Had to come here, all right? *Tia*'s the only, only family I got.

LEBÓN: And then Guapa shows up, outta nowhere, needin' to be saved, cuz it turns out, she's family somewhere too down the long-ass pike, and her step-dad's been sent to lock down, so we gotta be all pious and take good wholesome pity. And man, I got big heart. I love Guapa and everybody else. But what about us, man?

HAKIM: Huh?

LEBÓN: Pity US stuck here in this shit-town, crying our drunk asses for the good ol' days we ain't ever had, cause they're so far back we can't even remember.

HAKIM: Man, if Guapa heard you…

LEBÓN: I'm on her side, man.

HAKIM: Talk and talk, but you're sittin' here. Like a little slack-tivist.

LEBÓN: What [are] you-?

HAKIM: Slack-tivist. Thumbing through the net, signin' this petition and that, but I don't see you out on the street occupyin' anythin', takin' a real stand –

LEBÓN: Put YAKU up on that wall.

HAKIM: And they'll paint over it tomorrow. Haven't made a lick of difference.

LEBÓN: Got no idea.

HAKIM: You and all the rest… whine 'til doomsday, but they ain't EVER gonna try to do somethin' with their life.

LEBÓN: I'm doin'.

HAKIM: Fuckin' Quechua lessons on YouTube, for Chrissakes!

LEBÓN: [have] You seen Quechua in the [college] course catalogue?

HAKIM: Have you even looked?

LEBÓN: 10 million people in Colombia, Ecuador, Peru, Bolivia, Argentina and Chile speak it, but no. No. It don't count for them. If it ain't French, Italian,

German, Spanish, they got no room for indigenous languages. They're OUT of the picture. And it's Guapa's background, right? Learnin' not just cuz I wanna learn, but because she's here. I'm honorin.'

HAKIM: Slack-tivist.

LEBÓN: You just wanna eat your good colonial shit and be done with.

HAKIM: You're the one who eats shit.

LEBÓN: Yeah?

HAKIM: Man, you put it in a lid and you take it with you.

LEBÓN: Wanna hit me, bro? Come on. I can take.

HAKIM: Like you don't even know the history of Texas, man. You think it's ALL colonial right-wing shit we got and ever had goin' on down here? What about the marches, man? The cotton stamps and the New Deal? And the *bracero* rights people fought for? Think it's all oil barons, border patrol and homeland security? You got shit, bro, and that lid is full up to here.

LEBÓN: Yeah?

HAKIM: Fuck yeah.

LEBÓN: Show me what you got, *pendejo*.

HAKIM: …

LEBÓN: Or I'm gonna fuck your mama up the ass.

HAKIM: That's the best you can do?

LEBÓN: Fucking asshole.

HAKIM: That right?

LEBÓN: Fucking make-nice cocksucker.

HAKIM: All right.

Hakim hits him. LEBÓN retaliates. They fight, get real into it – out of rage, frustration and everything else.

HAKIM (CONT): Lousy piece of shit.
LEBÓN: Moron accountant motherfucker.
HAKIM: I'll tear you in half, *hijo-de-puta*.
LEBÓN:: Like you got any *cojones* to tear anything, *maricon*.
HAKIM: Don't you *maricon* me, man; I seen you giving that daddy head over on Bakers Street.
LEBÓN: Lying motherfucker.
HAKIM: Lie on me 'til it hurts, cocksucker.
LEBÓN: Cum in your goddamn mouth, *pendejo*.

They continue fighting. Roly walks in.

ROLY: What the fuck is going on here?

Breaking them up…

ROLY (CONT): Get up. Get up, you pieces of shit.
LEBÓN: Hey, Ma.
ROLY: Don't' "hey Ma" me, *cabroncito*. Don't wanna hear WORD from you. Making a mess of this place.
HAKIM: …Sorry.
ROLY: Is this all you can do: hit each other like little *cobardes* in some cage?
LEBÓN: …Is Guapa okay?
ROLY: I'm tired. Tired of ALL THIS SHIT.

A moment.

HAKIM: What'd doc say?

ROLY: Doc says what she says.

LEBÓN: …But Guapa…

ROLY: Not a word, *mi'jo. Aqui* you're gonna be silent from now on. Unless I say.

LEBÓN: Ma…

ROLY: Go to work. Do something for someone for a change.

LEBÓN: Do more than you think.

ROLY: Is that right?

LEBÓN: Look, Ma, it was an accident, okay? How many times I gotta-?

ROLY: OUT of my face!

LEBÓN walks away.

ROLY (CONT): And you better not get your *cholo* ass fired!

LEBÓN exits. A moment.

HAKIM: Want a coffee?

ROLY: She got head trauma….

HAKIM: …

ROLY: They say it's not uncommon in a fall. Lasts about twenty-four to forty-eight hours.

HAKIM: It'll go away, then.

ROLY: Got history.

HAKIM: …?

ROLY: Goes away, if you don't have history, but if…

HAKIM: What do you mean?

ROLY: Doc says she's suffered head trauma before.

HAKIM: When?

ROLY: Get me the tequila. Off the shelf there. …No. The good one. That's right.

HAKIM (*pressing, out of concern*): Like, playing in a game or something?

ROLY: When she was little…

HAKIM: What do you mean? What did she-?

ROLY: I don't know, Hakim. I don't know all that Guapa's gone through… At the end of the day, we don't really know anything about a person's life. .

HAKIM: …Want me to talk to the doctor? I'll go to the hospital. I know how to talk to these people. I did it when my ma was-

ROLY: Are you listening to me? I don't…I can't…

She drinks. A moment.

HAKIM: Is she walking at least?

ROLY: *shrugs*.

HAKIM: Good sign. Cause before…

ROLY: Shock. They say that happens sometimes. … She kept clutching her *estampita*. "Don't lose my Saint Thérèse, the little Flower. Keep her safe," she said. …

HAKIM: She'll be fine. You'll see.

ROLY: Gonna pray to the saints? Better send those prayers up fast, then, and throw in some cigars and gold coins while you're at it. …Aren't you gonna be late?

HAKIM: Huh?

ROLY: Work.

HAKIM: Don't want to-
ROLY: I'll be okay. Go on. Get yourself cleaned up. *(attempt to be playful, to lighten the mood)* You look like you've been in a fight.

He goes within. She drinks.
A moment.
She rises, turns on the radio. Radio blares in Spanish:

RADIO DJ (VO): *Siguiendo con noticias del mundo: Veinticuatro muertos, después de un secuestro express-*[24]

She immediately turns off the radio.

ROLY: *Desgraciada mierda.*

She drinks.
A moment.
Hakim re-enters. He's indeed freshened up a bit.

ROLY (CONT): Hey. You look nice.
HAKIM: In two minutes I'll be messed up all over again.
ROLY: But when you walk in to the diner-
HAKIM *(finishing her sentence)*: "Look your best." I know.
ROLY: *Pa que sufran!*
HAKIM: You sure you're gonna be-?

---

[24] Translation: Continuing with news of the world: Twenty four deaths after an express kidnapping [went sour]

ROLY: *(attempt to be playful, for his sake)* Me and *Patron* [tequila] here…we'll keep each other good company.

HAKIM: Don't get drunk, *Tia*.

ROLY: I'll be good. I promise.

HAKIM *(kisses her on the head)*: Love you.

ROLY: Love you back.

Hakim exits. She looks at whatever's been knocked about or moved in the fight.

ROLY (CONT): *Bueno, a limpiar!*

She cleans up. As she does so, she begins to sing in Spanish…

"Canción de Sangre/Blood Song"

ROLY: *Sangre de mi sangre*[25]
Dejadme en el olvido,
Que todo esta perdido
Desde que dijiste Adios.

Sangre de mi sangre,
Dejadme en tiniebla(s)
Que todo se quiebra
Desde que pediste perdón.
Sangre de mi sangre,

---

[25] Translation: Blood of my blood/Leave me in oblivion/Because all has been lost/Since you said Goodbye./Blood of my blood/Leave me in shadow/Because all has been broken/Since you said your So Long/Blood of my blood/

She is interrupted by Pepi, leading Guapa by the hand, as they enter.

PEPI (*to Guapa as they enter, mid conversation*): It's okay. We'll sit down in a bit.
ROLY (*drawing close*): *Ay*, Guapa…
PEPI: Leave her alone, Ma.
ROLY: *Pero que pasa?*
PEPI: She's tired.
ROLY: How do you feel, eh? Better? Treat you good at the hospital?
GUAPA: *shrugs.*
ROLY: She's not talking?
PEPI: She's not all that communicative, okay?
ROLY: But she understands, right? Guapa, you understand me?
PEPI: Don't get in her face!
ROLY: I'm not in her face. (*To Guapa*) What do the saints tell you?
GUAPA: …
ROLY: You pray to Saint Thérèse, the Little Flower. We'll all pray. And screw all the *pendejos* in this place… *Que se vayan todos pa la mierda!* … What?
PEPI: You're being weird.
GUAPA: *tugs.*
ROLY: *Que quieres?*
GUAPA: *kicks.*
ROLY: No. No *futbol* in the house.
GUAPA: *kicks.*
ROLY: What is it, Guapa?
GUAPA: *makes parched sound.*

ROLY: *Ay*, of course! I'm sorry. We'll get you some water! *(To Pepi)* Did they give you any medicine?
PEPI: Prescription won't be ready 'til tomorrow.
ROLY *(handing her water)*: Here you go.
GUAPA: *doesn't drink.*
PEPI: Am so exhausted. Just dealing with those assholes!
ROLY: They're not all assholes. That nurse lady was nice.
PEPI: Have so much homework to do.
ROLY: Get it done. I'll take care of Guapa.
PEPI: But you got your own-
ROLY: We ALL have our own stuff. But when someone's not well, we do our part.
PEPI: Did you call in sick at-?
ROLY: Getting one of the girls to cover some of my hours. I'll make them up once Guapa's all better.
PEPI: You know I could-
ROLY: Wanna get a scholarship to get your PhD in astrophysics? Focus on your studies. Leave the work to me. You worked enough at that stupid dead mall and everywhere else all through high school.
PEPI: *Ay*, Ma. You worry so much.
ROLY: I worry cuz I worry.
PEPI: Lebón at work?
ROLY: Sent him off. Can't look at him right now.
PEPI: Was an accident.
ROLY: There are no accidents, when you're doing something that you're not supposed
PEPI: … Here. It was in Guapa's pocket.
It's a peacock feather.

PEPI *(CONT, refers to feather)*: They said she asked for it. When they went to take the scan…

ROLY: *[Peacock feather]* Feels alive.

PEPI: …I'm sorry.

ROLY: What are you sorry for?

PEPI: It's my fault.

ROLY: Huh?

PEPI: … Shoulda just let him be. Lebón doesn't need me chasing him 'round town, seeing where he's at.

ROLY: You did what any sister-

PEPI: If I hadn't gone, then Guapa wouldn't have gone and we wouldn't be in this…

GUAPA: *kicks.*

ROLY: Shh. Shh.

PEPI (CONT): Could've tagged all night over at the old kindergarten, if I hadn't...

ROLY: It's all right.

PEPI: It's not all right. Don't keep saying it like it's gonna make everything better. I was there, Ma. I was the one who went looking for him because I was sick of having to cover for him all the time.

ROLY: You don't…

PEPI: Yes, I do. Cuz yeah, I'm a good sister and I want him to do good, and I know that he tries, and that in his own way he thinks he's doing the right thing, but how long has he been taggin? How many times have we told him? And he keeps on.

ROLY: Let me deal with…

PEPI: And the thing is, he's some kind of artist. Cuz that wall was… I mean, when I saw it, I was all angry and was gonna call him out on stuff, but...I just couldn't...Right?

GUAPA: *looks away.*

PEPI: Cuz it made me think of Abuela and the colorful flowers she used to have in her backyard and the kinds of stories she would tell us when we were little, and I started to think about all the stories that lived inside that old kindergarten, and all the stories we'll never know anything about, and how Lebon's *Yaku* – blazing in the night – might be the only thing that connects us to something that's even beyond Abuela and her stories...and Guapa was, like, "yeah, it's beyond beautiful, like the perfect book-movie in my head,"

GUAPA: *closes her eyes.*

PEPI: And we all started to get into it, like we wanted to be part of some story that was bigger than us, bigger than anything, - like we had wings or somethin' - even though we should have... I should have made us all come straight back home. Cuz somebody has to be responsible, right? Somebody has to...

A moment.

PEPI (CONT): ...Think she's sleeping.

ROLY: Bet she's just resting. Sick of all of us in this crazy, mixed-up house!

GUAPA: *opens her eyes.*

ROLY: Heard me, eh?

GUAPA: *slight smile.*

ROLY (to Pepi): ...Go on. Take a shower, do your homework.
PEPI: But...
ROLY: Nobody said you had to do everything.

A brief moment between them, and then Pepi starts to walk away.

ROLY (CONT): And remember to turn the knob. Or the water goes...
PEPI: Everywhere. I know.

Pepi goes within.
A moment.

ROLY: Gonna drink your water?
GUAPA: *looks away.*
ROLY: You're right. Tap water is *pura mierda* in this town.
GUAPA: *little laugh.*

Roly gets a carton or small jug of agua fresca from the fridge and pours it into a glass.

ROLY: I argue with Lebon, but he is right about that. I'll get you some juice. Good ol' jamaica[26]...
GUAPA: *moves her feet, making imaginary plays on the field.*

---

[26] Reference to Agua Fresca Jamaica (Hibiscus)

Roly observes, and hands her glass. Guapa sips.

ROLY: ...Listen, Guapa... I know this is...
GUAPA: *kicks.*
ROLY: But we're going to figure out a way to...
GUAPA: *kicks.*
ROLY: Have to be patient. Doc says these things....
GUAPA: *kicks.*
ROLY: *Tranquila!*
GUAPA: *quiet.*
ROLY: Know you're worried.
GUAPA: *shakes her head.*
ROLY: Of course you are. You're thinking about that game in Dallas and everything...
GUAPA: *shakes her head.*
ROLY: Well, why not? Don't you wanna play *futbol*?
GUAPA: *quiet.*
ROLY: Guapa, it's your game.
GUAPA: *quiet.*
ROLY: *Futbol-arte.* Isn't that what you call it?
GUAPA: *quiet.*
ROLY: Football-art. And it is, right? A kind of art. A little touch of the gods sometimes out there on the field.
GUAPA: *a slight look away.*
ROLY: Look, I may say a lot of things, but I won't let you give up. Between the saints and our pig-headed stubborn-ness, we'll get through this. We won't let Saint Thérèse, the Little Flower, say we didn't put up a fight!

Brief moment. Roly looks at the peacock feather.

ROLY: You know, Pepi always talks about her
Abuela…
But my Abuela, who lived even further away,
in a little house made of kindness and concrete,
my Abuela loved peacock feathers.
She used to collect them and put them in a big box,
one of those decorated wooden boxes
from a long, long time ago
where people kept their treasures.
She had maybe hundreds of feathers,
all stacked up in this box,
So that when you opened it,
you'd see this crazy burst of color,
like psychedelic almost.
She said each feather represented
a place she wanted to go.
I'd say "Abuela, but that's too many places!"
She'd give me a look,
one of those long looks only Abuelas can give,
And she'd say,
"There are so many places in the world.
Wondrous, strange, beautiful places.
How can you say it's too much, ni~na?"
And she'd let me stare at the feathers,
And tell me the places connected with each one.

Some were places she'd read about,
Some were places people in the family had been,
Some were just made up,

Which I thought wasn't fair,
Because how can you go someplace that's only in
your dreams?

And the feathers would fall from her hands
One by one,
Each one connected to a story, a place, memory....
And slowly, slowly, I'd open my fist,
And catch the feathers in my palms,
And let them tickle and caress me.
And then I'd toss them into the air,
And make a canopy
Of blues and greens,
Yellows and violets,
That felt as if it'd come from nothing:
Like we all come into this world.

Guapa reaches for the feather in Roly's hand.
Lights fade.

Scene Six

Exterior. Afternoon. Backyard of Roly's house. A few weeks later. Guapa is standing. Hakim has a soccer ball underfoot. Pepi and Roly sit, as if they were at a soccer game, acting as if they were in the crowd. They've been at this for a bit.

HAKIM: Okay, now you gotta pretend that I'm, like, waaaay far away, on the other side of the field, and it's like raining and shit
PEPI: Raining?

HAKIM: Why not? They play in the rain and snow and everything.

ROLY *(like a cheer)*: Okay, it's raining!

HAKIM: And it's second half, and it's tied 2-2, and the best forward on the opponent's team

ROLY: It's Barca[27] vs. Manchester, remember?

HAKIM: Is that what we-?

ROLY: Yes! We're Barca. And they're Manchester.

HAKIM: Okay. The best forward on Manchester's team just got a red card, cause he kicked one of Barca's players in the shins, like, really hard-

PEPI: Will you get on with it?

HAKIM: Anyway, this is a major point, like, super major. Understand?

GUAPA: *nods.*

HAKIM: And I look at you from across the field, waaay across, and I'm gonna…

He passes the ball. Guapa doesn't respond.

HAKIM (CONT): Maybe that was too much pressure. Tiebreaker point and all that. Let's try something else.

PEPI: This is so not working.

ROLY: Will you give it a rest?

PEPI: She doesn't wanna play.

ROLY: She's getting it. You're getting it, right?

GUAPA: *nods.*

HAKIM: Give her time.

---

[27] Barca is nickname used to refer to Futbol Club Barcelona. The pronunciation is Bar-sa.

PEPI: We can't push her. She's gonna freak out.
ROLY: Don't be [a] pessimist.
PEPI: I'm not, but-
ROLY: You have to go somewhere? Go, then. Text, whatever. *(to Guapa)* Vamos, Guapa. You can do this. Watch me.
HAKIM: What are you-?

Roly takes ball underfoot, and maneuvers it with familiarity, albeit a rusty one. She dribbles, gets a rhythm going.

PEPI: Ma. You're gonna confuse her.
ROLY: I know what I'm doing, *mi'ja. (to Guapa)* And you pretend you're Lionel Messi, right?
HAKIM: Or Marta.
ROLY: Or Marta or Ronaldo or Lucas Lobos *de los Tigres,* and you...

Roly executes a deft soccer maneuver, perhaps even a trick.

HAKIM: Way to go, *Tia!*
PEPI: Ma, where did you even learn that?
ROLY: I know some things. Besides, it's just playing, right?
PEPI: That's not just playing. That's-
ROLY: Leave me to my craziness. I'll leave you to yours. *(To Guapa)* See what I did, Guapa? See how easy?
GUAPA: *smiles.*

ROLY: You can do it. *(back in cheer mode)* Come on, Barca!

HAKIM: We'll take it slow, though.

ROLY: There's no rush here.

HAKIM: Okay, so let's set up a different kind of point situation. Let's say Barca's down a point.

ROLY: They would never-

HAKIM: They're not always ahead, *Tia.*

PEPI: I don't know.

ROLY: What is wrong with you now? ... Spit it out, *mi'ja.*

PEPI: ... Just think...

ROLY: What?

PEPI: Doc said we had to-

ROLY: *Me importa tres chingaos* what Doc says. Is she here? Does she know what she loves? If it was up to the Doc, she'd be moping around the house all day, staring at the ceiling.

HAKIM *(playful)*: Counting stars.

ROLY: What?

HAKIM *(playful)*: Like Pepi. Counting stars.

PEPI: I DO NOT count stars!

Guapa, as they've been discussing her, has started to dribble with the ball a bit. Some of the old freestyle moves coming back to her. Not full-out, but clearly, it's a start.

GUAPA: *a gesture.*

ROLY: *Qué?*

GUAPA: *a gesture.*

HAKIM: All right. We'll keep playing.

GUAPA: *a gesture.*
HAKIM: Yeah. Yeah. I'll go slow.
ROLY: See? She wants.
PEPI: "*Futbol* is freedom."
ROLY: What?
PEPI: That's what Bob Marley said.
HAKIM: He said "Football is Music."
PEPI: He said both. Want me to look it up?
GUAPA: *grunts.*
HAKIM: Sorry. Okay. So, let's say it's not a tiebreaker point, it's much earlier in the match, we're just getting our wind, sussing each other out, like who's gonna make what kind of move and why and-
GUAPA: *with feet, takes ball from him.*
HAKIM: Hey!

They play one on one.

ROLY *(shouting)*: Go, Barca! Show him what you got!
PEPI *(shouting)*: Make him sweat. Come on, Guapa!

They keep playing: Guapa is pushing herself to stay in the game, as well as pushing him. A test of her own strength and will.

ROLY: Look good, eh?
PEPI: She's gonna kick his ass.
HAKIM: No, she's not!
PEPI: Make him suffer, Guapa!
ROLY: Don't make him suffer too much. *Pobrecito.*
PEPI: He's strong as an ox.

HAKIM: Bull.

PEPI: What?

HAKIM (*in the one on one, midst all*): The expression...is...bull. Strong as a...

Guapa and Hakim are at each other: one has the ball, the other chases; one takes ball from the other with deft maneuver, the other tries to re-capture it, and so on. Their breathing and grunting, as they play, is like music.

PEPI: He's getting winded.

HAKIM: Am not!

ROLY: She's pushing herself too hard. Hakim, slow the heck down!

Guapa stays in the game. But she is pushing herself now. That's clear.

PEPI: Come on, make the goal! Pass him, pass him....

Guapa tries to make the pass and make a run for it. Hakim intercepts. She successfully re-captures the ball.

PEPI (*doing cheerleader moves*): Go, Guapa! Go, Guapa!

ROLY: WHAT are you doing?

PEPI: I can be a cheerleader.

ROLY: That's no kinda cheer I know.

PEPI: It's a Lady Gaga move. (*doing moves*) Go, Guapa! Go, Guapa!

Hakim, who has tried to block her, gives up now, totally winded, and catches his breath.

ROLY & PEPI: Go! Go!

Guapa runs.

ROLY & PEPI: Go! GO! GOOOOOOAL...

Guapa collapses.

ROLY *(goes to Guapa)*: Ay, Dios mio.
PEPI: What did I tell you? What did I?
HAKIM: I'll get some juice.

Hakim goes to kitchen.

ROLY: Come on. Breathe, breathe.
PEPI: She was doing better, too.
ROLY: And in, and out...

Hakim re-enters with juice, hands it to Roly, who tries to get Guapa to sip.

ROLY: Vamos. Drink.

Guapa sips a bit.

ROLY: That's right. Much better. You'll feel much better in no time.

Lebón enters.

LEBÓN: Hey.
PEPI: Hey.
LEBÓN: What's this?
HAKIM: We were just playing, and she just-
PEPI: Was totally kicking Hakim's ass, too.
LEBÓN: … Hey, Ma, want me to-?
ROLY: You've done enough!

Guapa coughs.

ROLY (CONT): A little more. Come on.

Guapa coughs.

PEPI: You're crowding her!
ROLY: What is it with you and "crowding?" I'm right here. Want me to be miles away?
LEBÓN: Gotta give her a little space. I know about these things.
ROLY: You're a Doc now? Don't see a diploma on the wall.
    Guapa coughs. A little more acutely this time.

HAKIM: I'll call the… [hospital].
GUAPA: *wordless cry.*

Brief moment.

ROLY: *Qué?*

GUAPA: *wordless shout.*

ROLY: …Don't have to call anyone, if you don't want. We can stay right here. *(To Guapa)* You beat his ass, that's what's important!

HAKIM: I was playing good.

LEBÓN: Regular Zidane, eh?

HAKIM: Look, when I get my game on, I'm warrior dude, okay?

LEBÓN: That what you call it?

HAKIM: Get off my ass.

LEBÓN: Didn't know I was on it.

HAKIM: Fuck you, man.

ROLY: *Oye*, are you two gonna start with THIS now? Cuz we don't need this, right? We don't need any-

GUAPA *(pronunciation: yah·**wahr**·chai)*: *Yawarchay.*

ROLY: …Qué?

GUAPA*(pronunciation: yah·**wahr**·chai, **roo**·p-hah·chee)*: *Yawarchay, ruphachiy.*

ROLY: What are you saying, child?

GUAPA*(pronunciation: yah·**wahr**·chai, **roo**·p-hah·chee)*: *Yawarchay, ruphachiy.*

LEBÓN *(translates)*: …To bleed, to burn.

GUAPA*(pronunciation: mahn·**chah**·kui)*: *Manchakuy.*

LEBÓN: To be afraid.

PEPI *(recognition)*: Quechua?

LEBÓN: Uh-huh.

Hakim, Pepi and Roly are witness now to the following:

GUAPA*(pronunciation: sah·**mah**·ree, **p'ah**·kee)*: *Samariy, p'akiy.*

LEBÓN: To breathe, to break.

GUAPA *(pronunciation: **wahm**·poo)*: Wampu.

LEBÓN: Boat.

GUAPA*(pronunciation: **ai**·chah **koor**·koo)*: Aycha kurku.

LEBÓN *(translates)*: Body.

GUAPA *(re-emphasing; pronunciation: **wahm**·poo, **ai**·chah **koor**·koo)*: Wampu, aycha kurku.

LEBÓN *(translates)*: Boat-body.

GUAPA *(pronunciation: **nah**·nai)*: Nanay

LEBÓN *(translates)*: Ache.

GUAPA *(pronunciation: pah·sahkh koo·tee·lyah, p'ah·**kees**·kah)*: Pasaq kutilla, p'akisqa.

LEBÓN *(translates)*: Always broken.

GUAPA *(pronunciation: **pah**·sahkh koo·**tee**·lyah, roo·p-hai)*: Pasaq kutilla, ruphay.

LEBÓN *(translates)*: Always burn.

GUAPA *(pronunciation: **sah**·pah)*: Sapa.

LEBÓN *(translates)*: Alone.

GUAPA *(pronunciation: **pah**·sahkh koo·**tee**·lyah, hokh, koo·**tee**·chee)*: Pasaq kutilla, huq, kutichiy.

LEBÓN *(translates)*: Always, another, to answer.

GUAPA *(pronunciation: mah·**nyah**·kui)*: Mañakuy.

LEBÓN *(translates)*: To ask for something.

GUAPA *(pronunciation: **pah**·sahkh koo·**tee**·lyah, hokh, ah·**tee**·pai)*: Pasaq kutilla, huq, atipay.

LEBÓN *(translates)*: Always, another, to bear.

GUAPA*(pronunication: **yah**·wahr)*: Yawar.

LEBÓN *(translates)*: Blood.

GUAPA: …

LEBÓN: …

GUAPA *(pronunciation: **pah**·sahkh koo·**tee**·lyah, hokh,
ee·nee)*: *Pasaq kutilla, huq,*
LEBÓN *(translates)*: Always, another,
GUAPA *(pronunciation: **p'ah**·kee)*: *P'akiy.*
LEBÓN *(translates)*: To break.

They shift now.

GUAPA: Before
LEBÓN *(translates into Quechua;(pronunciation: nyow
pahkh tah)*: ~nawpaqta
GUAPA *(in Spanish)*: *El decía*
LEBÓN: He would say
GUAPA: Stupid bitch.
…
ROLY: *Que dices, ni~na?*
GUAPA *(in Spanish)*: *El decia*
LEBÓN: He would say
GUAPA: "Dirt-and-mud-girl-stupid-bitch."
ROLY: Calm down.
GUAPA: *wordless shout*
ROLY: …
GUAPA *(in Spanish)*: *El decia*
"dirt-and-mud-girl-stupid-bitch"
(in Spanish) una y otra vez
until I
(In Quechua) iniy
LEBÓN: Believe.
ROLY: …

PEPI: Was this your step-dad?
GUAPA: I was six years old.
Thought
If Saint Thérèse, the Little Flower said

(quoting from memory)

"Let me be looked upon as one to be trampled underfoot"

GUAPA: Then
(In Quechua) Qhallu
LEBÓN: Tongue.
GUAPA: My *(in Quechua)qhallu* too.
My *(in Quechua) pachamuyu.*
LEBÓN: World.
GUAPA *(In Quechua)*: *t'aslara.*
LEBÓN: Map.
GUAPA: *Suti*
LEBÓN: Name.

GUAPA: "dirtandmudgirlstupidbitch."
He gave to me.
Thought
Lucky. To have *suti*
LEBÓN: Name.
GUAPA: Lucky
To have *tata.*
LEBÓN: Father.

GUAPA: *Santa Thérèse me va a proteger de todo,*
Porque ella es milagrosa y ella me mira,
Y ella no pregunta porque.

I let him call me, and thought, I'm dirt-and-mud.
There's nothin' else to me.
And we'd sit and watch Bruce Lee movies on the TV,
and my *tata* would laugh
and pour whiskey in my ear,
and I'd be: "Dad, déjà."
But he'd just laugh, and watch Lee, and say,
"See that, dirtandmudgirlstupidbitch?"
With a slap upside my head,
"That's what magic's like,"
While he took off his T,
and let his sweaty whiskey breath on me.

Thought
I'm lucky
Because some kids
don't even know what they're made of.
At least I know I'm dirt-and-mud.
HAKIM: Don't.
GUAPA: *Allichu.*
LEBON: Please.

GUAPA: *Pero algunas veces, algunas veces,*
I could feel these feathers inside of me.
Like, I had feathers,
instead of blue-green-and-white *venas* under my skin,
and I felt as if they could let me reach

those *futbol* cleats
hung up there on that telephone line near our house.
(as if calling to the heavens, in Quechua) Waira.
Janajjpacha.
LEBON: Air.
Sky.

GUAPA: And I thought one day
I'm gonna get to them,
those *futbol* cleats,
that have been always,
(In Quechua "always," pronunciation: pah·sahkh
koo·tee·lyah)
pasaq kutilla
been out of reach.
If I just…
Waira.
Janajjpacha.
Raphara.
LEBON: Air.
Sky.
Wing.
GUAPA: *Futbol.*
LEBÓN: Soccer.

They laugh.

GUAPA: To bloom
LEBÓN *(translates into Quechua; (pronunciation:*
<u>see</u>·sai): *Sisay.*

He looks at her with a sense of true recognition.

LEBÓN (CONT, *pronunciation:* **soo**·*mahkh*) *Sumaq.*
GUAPA (*translates*): Beautiful.

Scene Seven

Interior. Night. Roly's house. Some time later. A quiet has descended upon the house. The only thing that can be heard is the soft hum of night.

Roly wanders in, from within. She looks about. She's dead tired and yet restless at the same time. She grabs a kitchen rag, and rubs an area clean. She sets rag down. She opens a cupboard, and closes it. Random gestures. She's not sure what to do. She grabs the broom and sweeps. She sings softly to herself in Spanish, as she does so.

"Love's star (sweet bird of forgetting) " /"Estrella de amor (ave de olvido)"

ROLY: *No hay sol ni olvido*[28]
No hay canción que gritar
Deja caer tu sombra
Deja tu mar.
Porque dondequiera
Cantara felicidad

---

[28] Translation: There's neither sun nor loss/There's no song to proclaim/Let your shadow fall/Leave your ocean's trace/Because everywhere you go/happiness will reign/sweet bird of forgetting/Find your true day/ sweet bird of forgetting/let your peace sway.

Ave de olvido
Busca mi verdad.
Ave de olvido
Dame tu piedad.

Lebón walks in, from within.

LEBÓN: Should get some rest.
ROLY: Como *que* everybody is wandering the house tonight. What is this, Grand Central?
LEBÓN: Rest, Ma.
ROLY: Dust everywhere. *Pinche* Texas, always full of dust *dondequiera*.
LEBÓN: Guapa will be all right.
ROLY: You think she-?
LEBÓN: Yeah.
ROLY: After all she's been through… every time I think of that *cabron desgraciado de la mierda…*

She cleans: a way to release her rage. She perhaps hums the same little song she sang earlier under her breath.

LEBÓN: What's that song?
ROLY: *Yo que se.*
LEBÓN: One of Abuela's songs?
ROLY: Her songs, my songs, they all get mixed up together.
LEBÓN: Hey. Want a coffee?
ROLY: I'm already up. If I have a coffee, I'll be up all night and into the morning. Sometimes you come up with such things.

LEBÓN: Just like Dad, eh?

ROLY: Don't start with that. Give me a hand here. Can't reach.

LEBÓN: Corners. They're a bitch, right?

ROLY: My knees are shot.

LEBÓN (*cleans*): There.

ROLY: You sure?

LEBÓN: Know how to clean, Ma.

ROLY: Don't end up like me. I studied and studied and what? End up cleaning for a living. Just like my Ma. And not even like her, 'cause at least she had her own company for a while, was her own boss. I messed up my life, *mi'jo*. … Don't mean about having you, or Pepi, or taking care of Hakim and Guapa… YOU'RE my life. All of you… But mine…

LEBÓN: I know.

ROLY: What you know?

LEBÓN: I see things.

ROLY: Saints send you visions, too? Go on. Put this [rag] in the basket.

LEBÓN: What for?

ROLY: For the laundry, what for.

LEBÓN: But you barely used it.

ROLY: I am not having *microbios* around.

Lebón takes rag and puts it in laundry basket.

ROLY: Hear that?

LEBÓN: …?

ROLY: Birds waking.

LEBÓN: … Want me to take a look at the car in the morning? See if it's okay?

ROLY: That car is on its…

LEBÓN: Could still make it to Dallas.

ROLY: …*Y eso?* Going to the big game, too?

LEBÓN: Think Guapa should go, that's all.

ROLY: Barely got her game back.

LEBÓN: Could try, at least. she's been wantin' to go…

ROLY: Wanting and playing are not the same thing.

LEBÓN: Want her to get a chance at somethin.

ROLY: You sure you're talkin' about Guapa?

LEBÓN: …

ROLY: Okay, let's say we go… what happens when we get there? When they look at Guapa, if they look at her, and turn her right back 'round?

LEBÓN: Wouldn't do that.

ROLY: It'd be a wasted trip, and crying all the way back, and what's she gonna do with her life?

LEBÓN: …

ROLY: Believe me. I want her to do good. … After how that *cabrón desgraciado* treated her…It isn't right, y'know! … I had dreams too. Just like her when I was little.

LEBÓN: Futbol?

ROLY: Of running across some field, and making the best goal ever.

LEBÓN: You never-

ROLY: I was six years old. Wasn't good enough, fast enough. And slowly I let the dream fade… But I remember… how it felt to want something so much…

Brief moment.

ROLY: Really think they'll give her a chance?
LEBÓN: It's just Dallas.
ROLY: Players from all the different towns. And Guapa there. Right along with them…
LEBÓN: Showin' them off.
ROLY: Think she can?
LEBÓN: If they let her play, I bet she could find somethin' inside her to show them all the hell off. Even if just for a minute or two.
ROLY: … The look on their faces…
LEBÓN *(putting on voice of skeptical onlooker)*: What? That ol' chick pulling off that goddamn pass?
ROLY *(putting on another skeptical voice)*: Hell. That peasant girl ain't supposed to do that.

They laugh, but holding it in a bit, because it's late.

LEBÓN *(playful)*: Revenge of the dispossessed.
ROLY: Revenge of the *chingao chingados!*
LEBÓN: *Pues, chingate, amigo!*

They laugh again, a bit louder, trying to contain themselves.

ROLY: *Ay*, Lebón… You make me crazy sometimes.
LEBÓN *(playful)*: Only sometimes?
ROLY: *Ay*, it'd be good to see Guapa outrunning them on the field, teaching them all a thing or two about how to get by. Even if just for a little bit.

LEBÓN: And who knows? Maybe the saints will come down and give her a little push, send a *pinche* miracle her way.

ROLY *(a mixture of humorous flair and real sentiment behind it)*: Saint Therese, the little flower, help us make it to Dallas!

They laugh. Brief moment between them.

LEBÓN: I'm sorry, Ma.
ROLY: Huh?
LEBÓN: For cutting from work... and...
ROLY: As long as you don't...
LEBÓN: I promise.
ROLY: ... *Bueno.*
LEBÓN: Yeah?
ROLY: We're *yawar*, right?
LEBÓN: Learnin' Quechua too now?

Lebón gives her a light kiss on the head.

LEBÓN: Don't stay up too late.

Lebón goes within.
A moment.
Roly looks around. Little sigh of contentment.
She goes within.
Time shift; light shift.
Lights start to cross-fade into the next TRANSITION, as the radio is heard, in Spanish:

RADIO DJ (VO): *Este es el sol de la mañana en EL SOL, tu estación de estaciones, "La Favorita," aquí en radio dos, dos, punto cinco, FM: EL SOL.*[29]

On the radio: a bright four-note tune plays, the station's signature.

RADIO DJ (CONT, VO): *Y ahora seguimos con la ultima noticia: Se espera una ola de calor hoy después de una semana templada. Recomiendan tomar mucha agua y mantener las cortinas bajadas…*

Scene Eight

Interior. Day. Roly's house. Some time later.
Hakim is standing, dressed in simple futbol clothes. He's putting some snacks and such in a portable cooler. Perhaps he hums to himself as he does so.
Roly walks in, dressed nicely, purse in hand.

ROLY: *Vamos!* We're gonna be late, Guapa.
GUAPA *(from within, Off)*: *Ya voy!*
ROLY: We have to go to Dallas. And it's far.
HAKIM: Not that far.
ROLY: *Bueno*, it's far enough, and if we don' make it, it's gonna be a *tragedia* around here.

---

[29] Translation: This is your morning sun on THE SUN, your station of stations, "Your Favorite," here on radio two, two, point five, FM: THE SUN. … And now the latest news: A heatwave is expected today after a pleasant week. Drink lots of water and lower your windowshades…

Lebón enters, from outside.

LEBÓN: Where ARE you guys? We're gonna be late.
ROLY: Did you put gas in the car?
LEBÓN: Yes, Ma.
ROLY: Don't wanna have us running out of gas on the way.
LEBÓN: It's all taken care of.

Pepi enters, from outside.

PEPI: WHAT is going on? I've been in the car for, like, hours.
HAKIM: We're late.
ROLY: WE ARE NOT LATE. *(calling out)* Guapa! *Nos vamos!* If you wanna catch a bus, we'll see you there.
PEPI: Ma!
ROLY: If I don't say, she'll be all day…

Guapa enters, from within. She wears simple futbol jersey, shorts, and socks.

PEPI & HAKIM: Woo-hoo!
HAKIM: Look at Guapa!
PEPI *(doing her Lady Gaga cheerleader moves)*: Go, Guapa! Go, Guapa!

Perhaps the others also join in, following Pepi's lead with their "Go, Guapa! Go, Guapa" cheer.

GUAPA: Shut up. Can't find my cleats.

ROLY: That's why we've been waitin' here all this time?
PEPI: Had them the other day.
GUAPA: I'll borrow some when I get there.
ROLY: Can't do that. That's setting the wrong precedent.
GUAPA: Won't go, then.
ROLY: After we planned and planned and all the *sacrificios* and lamentations…
PEPI: Don't exaggerate.
ROLY: No. No. You are going. We are gonna figure this out.

They look. After little while…

LEBÓN: Did you look under the cleaning stuff?
ROLY: Why would I-?
LEBÓN: …
ROLY: What did you do now? What did you do?

Guapa retrieves a gift-wrapped shoebox from the area where the broom and such reside. She tears through the gift-wrap and opens the box, and reveals a new pair of cleats.

GUAPA *[In Quechua; translation: thank you]*: A~nay.

GUAPA hugs LEBÓN.

LEBÓN: Like Marta of Brazil.
PEPI: Like Guapa!

A huge embrace amongst all of them.

HAKIM: To Dallas!
GUAPA: Saint Therese, show us the way!
ROLY: And we'll show them how futbol is really played!

Epilogue

Exterior. Day. In suspended time. Image of seemingly endless road bathed in sunlight, the horizon line seems as if it is almost within reach. Instrumental music is heard: clean pure guitar lines along a driving yet gentle bass drone.

Guapa puts on her cleats, as images fade in and out on memory's evanescent track:
Sun's yearning upon the dry land;
An abandoned roadside Horchata stand with only the word LIME now visible;
An impossibly shiny road-stop filling station with a 24-Hour Mini Mart;
A lone telephone booth at one side of the filling station, a forlorn remnant of some other time;
A soccer field, as seen from above, the deep green pitch of the field beckoning;
A mural on a wall outside the soccer stadium, which reads FUTBOL = LIBERTAD, upon which is painted an image of a great big sun, which happens to be a soccer ball, surrounded by fierce (from the manner in which they've been drawn), bold stars;

and then, slowly, a close-up of a soccer ball in motion…

GUAPA: You've seen her.
She lives on this little strip between school and church
Just past the old dry cleaner's near Fiesta [market].
They call her Guapa, because she got no other name.
And even though she thinks it doesn't suit her,
She answers to it, anyway,
'cause it feels nice to be called Beautiful all day,

She's wearing new cleats that shine.
It's as if all the dirt and mud
has been rubbed out of her,
And in their place are pure, radiant feathers,
That lift her up,
And make her feel as if she could touch the sky
With her bare hands.

It's 1-1, and she's in the middle of the trick kick,
The one that she's been working on all this time,
When she can swear she sees the saints
Waving to her from the stands -
Saint Thérèse, the Little Flower,
And all the rest of them
from the shiny bottles over at Fiesta,
And with them, the faces of these other saints
whose names aren't in any book,
but who are with her, here, too,
just like the Little Flower is,
and their names are Roly, Pepi, Lebon, and Hakim,

Roly, Pepi, Lebon, Hakim appear.

and all of them, all of them,
Are doing a WAVE as she takes hold of the ball,
As she runs with the pulse of ancient blood
That sings out in her mother's tongue:
(pronunciation: sah·mah·ree)   *Samariy*
(pronunciation: hokh·mahn·tah)   *huqmanta*
(and she translates) To breathe again.

She's spent most of her life dreaming about *futbol*,
Even though it's kinda crazy,
And people make fun,
And she probably doesn't have any real chance
at it anyway.
So what if the sun blinds her eyes?
So what if she's gotta work twice as hard
to make the shot?
It's a beautiful game. *"Football-art,"*
And for Guapa, that's enough.

Image of the soccer ball moving closer and closer…

End of play

Caridad Svich-Bio:

Caridad Svich received a 2012 OBIE Award for Lifetime Achievement in the theatre, and the 2011 American Theatre Critics Association Primus Prize for her play *The House of the Spirits*, based on the Isabel Allende novel. She has been short-listed for the PEN Award in Drama four times, including in the year 2012 for her play *Magnificent Waste*. In the 2012-13 season: 2012 Edgerton Foundation New Play Award round two recipient *GUAPA* received a rolling world premiere courtesy of NNPN at Borderlands Theater in Arizona, Miracle Theatre in Oregon and Phoenix Theater in Indiana; her 4-actor play *Love in the Time of Cholera*, based on the Gabriel Garcia Marquez novel, premiered at Repertorio Espanol in NYC, where it is still running, *The Tropic of X* premiered at Single Carrot Theatre in Baltimore. Her play *Spark* received 32 readings across the US and abroad, including a reading at the Cherry Lane Theatre produced by TEL and Mannatee Films under Scott Schwartz' direction in November 2012 to honor female war veterans (http://www.nopassport.org/spark).

Among her key works: *12 Ophelias, Any Place But Here, Alchemy of Desire/Dead-Man's Blues, Iphigenia Crash Land Falls on the Neon Shell That Was Once Her Heart (a rave fable), Instructions for Breathing, Magnificent Waste* and the multimedia collaboration *The Booth Variations*. Five of her plays radically re-imagining ancient Greek tragedies are published in the September 2012 collection *Blasted*

Heavens (Eyecorner Press, University of Denmark). Her works are also published by TCG, Broadway Play Publishing, Playscripts, Arte Publico Press, Smith & Kraus, Alexander Street Press, and more.

Among her awards/recognitions are: Harvard University Radcliffe Institute for Advanced Study Fellowship TCG/Pew Charitable Trusts National Theater Artist Residency at INTAR, NEA/TCG Playwriting Residency at the Mark Taper Theatre Forum Latino Theatre Initiative and a California Arts Council Fellowship. She has edited several books on theatre including *Out of Silence: Censorship in Theatre & Performance* (Eyecorner Press), *Trans-Global Readings* and *Theatre in Crisis?* (both for Manchester University Press) *Divine Fire* (BackStage Books), and *Out of the Fringe: Contemporary Latina/o Theatre & Performance* (TCG), and *Conducting a Life: Reflections on the Theatre of Maria Irene Fornes* (Smith & Kraus). Her translations of Federico Garcia Lorca's plays are collected in *Lorca: Six Major Plays* (NoPassport Press) and *Impossible Theatre* (Smith & Kraus). She has also translated theatre works by Julio Cortazar, Lope de Vega, Calderon de la Barca, Antonio Buero Vallejo and contemporary plays from Mexico, Cuba, Serbia and Catalonia.

She is alumna playwright of New Dramatists, founder of NoPassport theatre alliance & press (http://www.nopassport.org), Drama Editor of *Asymptote* journal of literary translation, associate editor of Routledge/UK's *Contemporary Theatre Review* and contributing editor of *TheatreForum*. She is affiliated artist of the Lark Play Development Center, Woodshed Collective, New Georges, and a Lifetime member of Ensemble Studio Theatre.

She holds an MFA in Theatre from UCSD, and she trained for four consecutive years with Maria Irene Fornes at INTAR. She has taught playwriting at Bard College, Barnard College, Bennington College, Einhorn School of the Arts at Primary Stages, OSU, Rutgers University-New Brunswick, ScriptWorks, UCSD, and Yale School of Drama. She is an entry in the *Oxford Encyclopedia of Latino Literature*. Website: http://www.caridadsvich.com